Angel returned to the inferno.

In all, he went back into the building eleven times, bringing out one or two people on every trip. After the fourth time, the neighbors began to applaud him each time he returned, and the lady with the hose started watering him down every time she saw him. Finally, they assured him that everyone was out and accounted for. Sirens grew closer—he thought it was too late to save the block, but still, the fire needed to be contained before it spread to other buildings. Angel was tired, his hair singed, flesh and clothing scorched. But he had accomplished something.

He left the crowd behind and went back around the building, heading for the freeway and the car he had left there.

But before he reached it, five men emerged from the shadows, heavily armed and bearing wooden stakes.

"No one could've done all that," one of them said. "At least, no one human."

Angel™

Available from Simon Spotlight

The Essential Angel Posterbook

Available from Pocket Books

For Chris, who got me into this

Historian's Note: This book takes place in the fourth season of *Angel*.

First Simon Spotlight Entertainment edition October 2004

SSE

SIMON SPOTLIGHT ENTERTAINMENT

An imprint of Simon & Schuster Children's Publishing Division

1230 Avenue of the Americas, New York, New York 10020

™ & © Twentieth Century Fox Film Corporation. All Rights Reserved.

All rights reserved, including the right of reproduction in whole or in part in any form.

SIMON SPOTLIGHT ENTERTAINMENT and colophon are registered trademarks of Simon & Schuster.

Manufactured in the United States of America

First Edition 10 9 8 7 6 5 4 3 2 1

Library of Congress Control Number 2004102537

ISBN 0-689-87085-X

ANGEL ™

love and death

Jeff Mariotte

An original novel based on the television series
created by Joss Whedon & David Greenwalt

SIMON SPOTLIGHT ENTERTAINMENT
New York   London   Toronto   Sydney

ACKNOWLEDGMENTS

Thanks are due to a variety of folks who helped with this book and with life in general, including—but not limited to—Maryelizabeth Hart, Holly and David Mariotte, Cindy Chapman, Tara O'Shea, Cari Kinz, Christopher Golden, Scott Ciencin, Jack Passarella. Special thanks to Tricia and Patrick and Beth and Debbie and Joss and David. And the rest of you. You know who you are.

PROLOGUE

Five Nights Ago

"Listen up and listen good, ladies and gents, because the sun has gone down over the horizon and the darkness has enveloped this land, from sea to whining sea, and that means we're in the Night Country now. I'm Mac Lindley, your guide and host for the Night Country, and for those of you in the wilds of Montana or, say, New Jersey who just now figured out how to work your radios, this is what it's all about. I'll share some information, I'll try to entertain, I'll take your calls and your e-mails, and together we'll explore the Night Country. We'll figure out where the danger lies and where the truth is. I'll steer you right and I'll say what's what—you can always count on that from Mac Lindley, if nothing else. So welcome to the show, and let's see what you've got on your minds out there."

Mac turned away from the microphone and allowed himself a quick sip of coffee. There'd been a time when he had an engineer running the controls who'd have grabbed the pod and muted the mic long enough for him to swallow. *Engineer would have screened the calls, too,* he thought, *weeding out the cranks and nutballs*.

That had been a long time ago. Now, if it weren't for cranks and nutballs, he'd have no audience at all. That was okay with him. They were his people. The Night Country was Mac Lindley's kingdom, and he was happy on its throne. He was one of them, after all. He had spent decades looking for his niche, and he'd finally found it a few years back when the idea for the Night Country had occurred to him.

Mac figured he had a face made for radio. The various parts didn't seem like they'd been tooled for the same person—he had an old man's honker of a nose, for instance, but a younger, smaller man's neat, precise ears, and his eyes were a strange color, almost gold, but with perfect 20-20 vision. His teeth were remarkably straight, as well, convincing most people he met that he'd had braces, although he never had. But his teeth were contained within a mouth that didn't live up to their perfection: lips that were too narrow and too red, and shaped in a kind of perpetual downturned frown.

"For instance," he continued, turning back to the microphone, "here's an e-mail from Garth in Elmyra. 'Hi, Mac—longtime listener here. What I'd like to know is what you consider the greatest threat to our way of life. Thanks, Garth.' Well, Garth, that's a good question, and of course there are lots of answers. Terrorists, naturally, and dope fiends who'll kill you for the twenty bucks in your wallet so they can stick a needle in their arms or score that next hit of crack or OxyContin. Heart disease and cancer are at the top of the list, of course, though if you've been listening awhile you know old Mac beat the Big C when it came his way. Alcohol is up there, too, especially when it mixes with automobiles.

"But for my money—and some of you are gonna be shaking your heads when I say this, and I'll tell you right now, don't bother e-mailing me to say I'm buggier than your aunt Irma because I've already heard it all—for my money, I've got to say the biggest threat we're facing today is Los Angeles. The City of Angels.

"I know what you're thinking. You're thinking old Mac has become one of those cultural crusaders, and what I'm talking about here is the spew of waste that comes out of Hollywood, those terrible movies and TV shows full of filth and human degradation. And those are bad, but that's not the threat I'm referring to. Not at all. Because this is

3

the Night Country, and there's no whining allowed here, and what I'm talking about is the fact that L.A. has become a supernatural cesspool, crawling with vampires and demons and ghouls and ghosties. The night is busier than the day in L.A., and that's a fact.

"And what you have to understand about these creatures, especially vampires, is that they breed like rabbits. Worse. Just look at it realistically. Vampires have to feed on human beings to survive, right? And when they feed, their victims then become vampires too. And *they* have to feed, and so on. So if you start with one and he feeds once a night, at the end of that first week you then have seven new ones. They each feed once a night, too, so at the end of week two— and I'm simplifying the math here, because really the one turned on Monday is going to be feeding on Tuesday, and so on—at the end of week two you've got forty-nine going. Week three, that's three hundred and forty-three. Week five, you're up over sixteen thousand. And so on, and so on."

Mac turned away from the mic again and stifled a yawn. This would be another long night. They all were. He hadn't been sleeping well lately. He slept daytimes, worked nights—*just like those vampires I talk about*. But recently he'd been having a harder time sleeping, had been troubled by bad dreams, daymares, and every little noise outside seemed to disturb his uneasy rest.

"It's a plague, it's a pox, it's a curse. It's worse than all those other things I mentioned put together. And it may have taken root in L.A., but it won't stay there, any more than L.A.'s other plagues—tabloid TV, dramedies, Crips and Bloods, and those dinner plates with maybe two beans and a piece of meat no bigger than your thumbnail, with a little red sauce drizzled over it—have stayed there.

"You wanted to know the truth, Garth, and that's why you tuned in to the Night Country. There it is. The truth is that L.A. is a time bomb, and when it blows we'll all go down. If I were you, ladies and gents, citizens of the Night Country, I'd load up on wooden stakes and silver bullets and get myself out to Los Angeles. Fix this problem before it spreads, before it's too late for any of us.

"People, it's open season on monsters. Get out there and collect some trophies."

CHAPTER ONE

Tonight

Angel checked his map again. Not because his memory was failing with age—if that had been in his cards, it likely would have happened 160 years ago—but because he wasn't entirely sure he trusted the map. Fred had printed it from one of those online mapping sites, and Angel figured it was a safe bet he had been in more parts of Los Angeles than her computer had—or anyone else's computer, for that matter. And it was entirely possible that whoever had programmed that mapping function had never set foot in the city.

According to the tiny color map Fred had printed out for him, with the purple line that was supposed to indicate his route, he was just a half-mile from the Fletcher home in the Beverly Glen section of town. Houses in this area were few and far between, perched on hillsides overlooking the city, connected by winding roads barely wide enough for two cars to go around each other. Streetlights were few as well, and the thickly treed hills were dark, with only the car's headlights and the glow from the occasional house illuminating his way. That was okay; Angel could see in the dark almost as well as he could in bright daylight, and since bright daylight had the additional disadvantage of causing him to burst into flames—vampire occupational hazard—he really preferred the dark of night.

He wasn't at all sure what to expect when he found the place. Herman Fletcher had called the Hyperion Hotel a couple of days before, asking for help with some kind of supernatural presence at his house. That, in itself, wasn't surprising; Angel and his comrades had developed a bit of a reputation—even though they'd tried to keep it low-key—as the go-to people when things that went *bump* in the night started to go *chomp* as well. At first, Mr. Fletcher had been pretty casual about the whole thing, as if whatever was going on wasn't really any big deal, and Angel had agreed to drop by when he had a chance. But tonight Mr. Fletcher had called back in a near panic. And according to Lorne, who'd taken the call, Mr. Fletcher's story had been a bit light on details.

"I can't get a handle on what kind of problem they've got," Lorne, a Pylean demon who was part of Angel Investigations, had said. "Fletcher seemed a little on the sketchy side, if you know what I mean, like he's seen a few too many bad movies on the late show and gotten them confused with real life, or what passes for it. He said something about blood dripping from the walls, but then mentioned blood pouring from the faucets, and you know those two hardly ever go together. And with the weak cell signals up in those hills, I couldn't tell if he said chains were rattling in the attic or he was getting rattled by chimps in his attic. Bats in the belfry would be my guess, although purely on the metaphorical level, of course. The only thing I'd swear to is that he sounded as scared as the investors in the next Ben Affleck–J.Lo movie."

"I'll check it out," Angel had said. He hadn't added that the mood in the hotel was so tense, he was happy to get away—even if it turned out that what the Fletchers really needed was a plumber and not a vampire. Fred and Gunn were not quite at each other's throats but, possibly worse, they were giving each other the silent treatment—which, after months of cooing and lovey-dovey talk, was extremely hard to take. Wesley—who had been keeping his distance ever since kidnapping Angel's son, Connor—had started coming around the hotel again, giving Angel the difficult choice of tearing his throat out or ignoring him. So far, he'd opted to ignore. Cordelia had been spending most of her time away, off someplace with Connor, which grated on Angel. *Sure*, he thought, *she's closer to his age, but only because everyone alive is closer to his age than mine.* Lorne, natural peacekeeper that he was, tried to run interference between everyone and everyone else, and the effort was grinding on him, wearing out even his legendary patience.

So a night in the hills? Possibly with the opportunity to punch something a lot? Kind of a blessing.

Reaching an intersection, he peered through the darkness at a street sign, looking for Oak Tree Lane. *Okay, maybe I don't get up this way as often as I might,* he thought. *It's a big city, after all.* On this small side street there were a few houses standing close together, with a narrow alley running behind them. But it wasn't Oak Tree, so he was about to drive on when a flurry of motion in the alley caught his eye. He pressed down on the brake and took a closer look.

At first glance, it looked like a man was attacking a woman. That was enough to demand Angel's intervention, especially since the man was well over six feet tall and brawny, and the woman was barely five feet, slender, and obviously terrified. She wore a hooded sweatshirt and white shorts, like tennis shorts. Somehow, her bare legs made her look especially vulnerable. She had backed up against the fence behind one of the homes, standing close to a couple of plastic garbage cans as if they could offer her shelter or aid. The man advanced in a near crouch, his arms out to grab her. Obviously, Angel had happened along just in time.

But as he got out of his GTX and ran a little closer, Angel noticed something else: The man had the elongated fangs, ridged forehead, and clawed hands of his own kind. *Vampire!* Although not, he was convinced, the kind with a soul—Angel was alone in that regard. He yanked a stake from beneath his coat and charged into the alley. The smell of vampires was thick here. *But not for long . . .*

When the other vamp spotted Angel, he turned away from his prey and smiled. "Oh, good," he said happily. "Seconds. I *am* famished tonight."

"I'm not your dinner," Angel replied. "I'm your worst nightmare." *Okay, cliché,* he thought, *but it's short notice.* He was surprised the vampire hadn't recognized him yet. Most of the city's bloodsuckers at least knew of Angel, and avoided him when they could.

The vamp called him on it. "Snappy dialogue too," he said, still grinning. He wore a navy blue T-shirt with the name of a sporting goods manufacturer on it, jeans, and sneakers. "You don't disappoint."

So the vampire *did* recognize him. But Angel wasn't afraid, though the situation was getting stranger by the second. He didn't worry about it, as he had moved within striking range. The vamp waited for him, legs spread for balance, clawed hands ready. Angel felt the comforting, smooth curve of the well-turned wooden stake in his fist and watched for an opening.

A sound behind him distracted, but only for a moment. The woman—running away, no doubt. But the noise grew louder, the flutter of fabric, soft footfalls—she was getting closer, not farther, and then he realized that her scent was all wrong too. *She* was a vamp as well. Angel didn't want to turn away from his initial foe, but he hazarded a quick glance just in time to see her diving toward him, fangs extended.

At the same time, the male vamp rushed him.

Angel braced himself for impact, bending forward at the waist as the female leaped onto his back, bringing the stake around under his left arm. He turned slightly to his left at the same time so that as she landed, she would slide that way, exposing her heart. Her claws dug through his coat and shirt into his flesh, but he drove the stake up and into her before her fangs reached him. *Should have worn the leather duster,* he thought. *It wouldn't have torn so easily.*

She fell away, and Angel was already moving

again, whipping the stake back around to meet the launched assault of the male. Angel ducked under the airborne attacker, raising his shoulder up to catch the vamp in the chin and shoving the stake up into his heart at the same time. The vamp uttered a quick groan and dropped to the ground behind Angel.

Angel turned around, surveying the scene. The male and female vamps were both lifeless on the ground, but neither had erupted into the spray of dust that they should have. *This doesn't make any sense,* Angel thought. A vampire doesn't just die—it *disintegrates* when a wooden stake penetrates its heart. If the stake had somehow missed both hearts—and Angel had dusted enough vamps to know when he had struck home—they would merely be injured, and they'd still be fighting him.

The only possible answer was that he hadn't missed their hearts—and that they weren't vampires.

He edged closer to the male's still form. His fangs remained visible, his telltale forehead still clearly on display. Angel dropped to a squat, carefully extending one hand toward the vamp. If he was only faking, Angel wanted to be ready to defend himself. He needed to find out what was going on—he didn't like being wrong about something like vampires. And, he remembered, he had smelled vamps as soon as he'd approached. His nose wasn't easily fooled.

But before his outstretched hand touched the lifeless form in front of him, it shimmered, as if from intense heat, and then vanished completely. Stunned, Angel looked toward the female, who was disappearing as well.

Angel stood alone in the alley, wondering what had become of the two seeming vampires, and why they had set what appeared to be a trap for him in the first place, since he couldn't imagine any reason for this strange situation except as a trap.

The Fletcher house.

He had nearly forgotten why he had come this way in the first place. The Fletchers. He had allowed himself to be distracted by these vanishing vamps, while whatever danger had so upset Herman Fletcher went unchallenged. No time to stick around here trying to figure out what had happened and why—he had urgent business elsewhere. He ran back to the car as lights began to flicker on inside some of the houses, the sounds of the short battle having roused the inhabitants. Someone would probably call the police, who would arrive and find exactly nothing.

When he cranked the engine, the radio came on, playing the last few bars of the Rolling Stones' "Sympathy for the Devil." *Hope that's not an omen,* Angel thought. He peeled away from the shoulder on which he'd parked, still looking for Oak Tree Lane.

He found it a couple of streets later, and made a hard right turn, the car's rear wheels fishtailing on the gravelly shoulder. The Fletcher house was three quarters of a mile up the hill, on the right. It was a medium-size California ranch house, single-storied and low-slung, with a gently sloping roof and a wide porch in front, set back from the road by a big lawn that was dotted here and there with spreading live oaks. Lights burned inside, bathing the grounds through many-paned windows. He went up the long driveway and parked in a broad, circular driveway.

Angel still hadn't quite shaken off the uncomfortable feeling that had settled over him in that alley— the idea that he had been set up for something, but didn't know what. If the intent was to create a diversion, to delay his arrival here, then it had worked. That idea filled him with dread. He had simply wanted to help these people, and if he had somehow allowed harm to come to them . . .

No good thinking like that. He tried to shake off the thought, like a dog coming out of a lake, and walked up a couple of steps to a solid wooden door. A doorbell button glowed softly to the right. Angel pressed it and heard a sonorous chime from deep within the house. He waited a few moments and, hearing no movement from within, he pushed it again.

Still nothing. He banged on the door with his

fist. When there was no response to that, he called Herman Fletcher's name. Finally, he tried the door. Unlocked, it opened at his touch.

Now the moment of truth. As a vampire, Angel couldn't enter a home uninvited—as long as its occupants were alive. He shouted Fletcher's name into the hardwood-floored entryway, and then, hoping to feel the familiar invisible barrier, stepped across the threshold.

But there was no barrier, no force preventing his entry. Which made it official: The Fletchers were dead.

Angel stood very still on the wooden floor, listening. If whatever had killed them had come from within the house, as Mr. Fletcher's phone calls had seemed to indicate, then it could still be here. Still malevolent, maybe still hungry. Angel had survived for going on 250 years; he was a lot tougher, no doubt, than Herman Fletcher and his family, but part of that survival came from not taking stupid chances unnecessarily. He was walking into a house of death—he would only do so with great caution.

The Fletchers had lived in a very middle-class manner, Angel saw, especially considering the upscale neighborhood that surrounded them. The few furnishings in this entryway—a side table, a chandelier, some framed pictures on the wall— were plain. The side table was rough-hewn wood, the chandelier glass and gold paint, the pictures merely posters in inexpensive metal frames. At the back of the foyer was a coat closet, and open doorways led off in both directions. Not hearing anything in either, Angel picked his left and passed through into a living room that could have housed the Cleavers or just about any other sitcom family of the last century.

Except that here, the sense of middle-class comfort was shattered by the carnage that greeted him. Furniture had been upended, legs snapped off of chairs, the upholstery slashed on a sofa, with the stuffing pulled out. Fancy white textured wallpaper hung from the walls in ribbons. The glass top of an end table had been smashed into a hundred pieces. Just walking through the doorway, Angel felt a strange, disquieting sensation, as if some malevolent presence was breathing down his neck, just on the other side of a thin veil that kept it from being seen or touched.

In the middle of it all was a man whom Angel took to be Herman Fletcher. Or what was left of Herman Fletcher, anyway. His head rested against one wall, eyes open and facing the door as if he were waiting for someone. But his body was a dozen feet away, chest ripped open. Fresh blood soaked the discount carpeting, filling the room with a familiar and tantalizing metallic scent. Angel glanced into the chest cavity and saw that it seemed to be a few organs short, but he found them a moment later, still warm, lying on the surface of a wooden sideboard as if someone had planned to serve them later with brandy and cigars.

Angel shuddered. Whoever—or whatever—had done this to Mr. Fletcher had taken its time, and had seemingly enjoyed the work. And this was just one member of the family—When Mr. Fletcher had called, he'd implied that there was a Mrs. Fletcher and some kids in the house.

Angel searched the rest of the house, eventually finding what he believed to be all the victims. Mrs. Fletcher had been killed in the master bedroom. He found an adolescent son in the basement, where he had apparently been building a model, pieces of which were now embedded in his flesh. And a teenage daughter was in two rooms, the upper half of her body in her bedroom and the lower half in the adjoining bath, a river of blood connecting them.

In each room, the destruction was nearly total. And in each, Angel felt the same shiver on his spine. Something was here, with him, he was sure, watching his every move. He couldn't see it, couldn't smell anything except the stink of bloodshed and death, couldn't hear a sound but his own footsteps. He tried speaking to it, but got no answer. His fists clenched, wanting to hit something.

But there would be no satisfaction tonight, he was sure. Whatever the presence here was, it kept its distance, not revealing itself to Angel. It had done its dirty work and then had gone back into hiding.

Worse, it had kept Angel distracted long enough to finish what it had started. He was sure, now, that the vampire brawl he'd interrupted had been nothing but a diversion meant to slow him down.

And you fell for it, he chastised himself. *Instead of keeping your eye on the ball, you were played for a sucker.*

That makes you just as responsible for these people's deaths as whatever force did them in.

CHAPTER TWO

Having searched the house from top to bottom, Angel couldn't find any more bodies, or any sign of who—or what—had killed the Fletchers, beyond the indefinable presence that he felt. Finally, he gave up and drove back down the hill to the alley where he'd fought the two vampires. *Or non-vampires, to be more precise*, he thought. *They looked like vamps, but they sure didn't die like them.* If the police had come, they hadn't stayed.

He spent almost thirty minutes combing the alley for any clues, but came up empty-handed. It was as if his opponents had never existed. There was no blood on the ground from where he'd stabbed them, no stray threads that he could identify as having come from their clothes. Neither one had conveniently dropped a wallet containing a name and address.

All in all, the evening had been a total washout, and it made Angel angry—at himself more than at anything else. He had a lot to atone for: decades of killing without a second thought; drinking the blood of innocents for his own sustenance and, he had to admit—at least in his darker moments—for his own pleasure. After he'd been cursed with a soul, he had eventually come to realize what most vampires never could: that his existence had been harmful, destructive, and that the world would have been a better place if he had never been born.

But since he had, and since there was no undoing the crimes he had committed, he had set himself the goal of redeeming himself through good works, of battling the darkness and those, like himself, who took advantage of it to prey upon the weak. He had found allies in the struggle and had banded with them, but now they had struggles of their own to deal with, so he had come out alone to the Fletcher house.

Too little, too late.

In a black temper, he gave up and headed back down the hill.

Whenever something horrible happened in Los Angeles, Angel knew some consideration had to be given to the theory that law firm Wolfram & Hart—or, at the very least, one of the firm's clients—was behind it.

At this hour, the downtown high-rise the firm occupied would be mostly dark, and locked up tighter than the proverbial drum. That didn't mean Angel couldn't get into it; he had proven many times that he could. But on this occasion, he doubted breaking in would do him any good. It wasn't likely that he'd find anyone he knew on the premises, and it was always easier to shake information from those with whom he'd already dealt than from new people, who often believed that the might of the firm would protect them from Angel's wrath.

So instead of heading there, he went to a different downtown high-rise and pounded on the door of Wolfram & Hart attorney Lilah Morgan. She worked late many nights, but she'd be home by now. Angel didn't really know—or care—if she had a social life, but he figured she was generally too busy trying to claw her way up the firm's hierarchy to spend her time socializing after her long work days.

Angel waited impatiently in the hallway until the door opened about four minutes later. Lilah, wearing a white silk robe over a sheer blue nightgown, her thick brown hair mussed from bed, looked at him with sleepy eyes. "Oh," she said. "It's you. *Quel* surprise."

"May I come in?" Angel asked.

Lilah shrugged. "No. Anything you have to say to me can be said from right there."

"Fine with me," Angel said. "It's not my neighbors who'll be disturbed."

Lilah arched one eyebrow. "I don't like my neighbors, anyway."

"Not evil enough for you?"

"Not by half. What brings you here, Angel? Surely you didn't come just to interrupt my beauty sleep."

"You're in bed early," Angel observed. "Must take a lot out of you, working so hard to protect the rights of murderers and demons."

Lilah started to close the door. "Angel, If you came just to judge me, make an appointment with my secretary. I only accept absurd criticism during working hours."

"That must keep your schedule jammed," Angel pointed out. "But I'm actually here with a specific question. And—even though you may not think so, because I'm talking to *you*—I want the truth. You know if I find out you lied to me, I can make your life difficult."

"You're *so* not my concern anymore, Angel. But go ahead, ask your question. If it doesn't cost me anything to not lie to you, then I won't."

"Good to know. Here it is: There was a family murdered tonight, up in Beverly Glen. Four people—"

Lilah casually held up her hands to stop him. "The Fletchers," she said.

"You already know about it, then?"

She huffed and ran her fingers through her hair. "Not because we had anything to do with it. I've already had two calls about it since I got home this evening. The senior partners don't like it when plainly supernatural murders happen on their turf without their knowledge or consent. I've already got some feelers out, and I have to go in early tomorrow to start preparing my report."

Angel studied the devious lawyer. She didn't exhibit any of the usual giveaways of a liar: the sideways glances, the shuffling feet, the pausing to keep a story straight. She spoke clearly and looked straight into Angel's eyes. By every indication, she *seemed* to be telling the truth.

Which is probably a required seminar at Wolfram & Hart, he thought. *Convincing lying for dummies.*

She read his gaze. "You can believe me or not, Angel. Trust me, it really makes absolutely no difference to me. If you can come up with some convoluted rationale why I'd be lying to you about this, well then, by all means go ahead."

"No special reason," Angel said. "Except that I just generally don't trust you."

"Then why knock on my door?"

Angel shrugged. "I like to keep you on your feet, let you know I'm still out here."

Lilah grinned, but it was not a friendly grin.

More like one a mouse might toss out to a cat after it was safely in its hole. "Oh, joy. Are you leaving now? That would truly improve my night."

"I'll leave," Angel said. "You really don't want me to find out you've been lying to me. And if you do learn anything about the murders? Let me know. I'm taking a personal interest."

"So noted," Lilah said. "Same goes for you—if you come up with any answers, I'd appreciate a heads-up. The sooner I can make a report, the better it'll be."

"Sure," Angel said, already turning away to head back to the elevator. It hadn't been an entirely wasted trip. At least it confirmed his suspicion that there was a supernatural element to the Fletcher murders, that it hadn't simply been the work of some madman. He knew there wasn't a chance in the world that he'd report any findings to Lilah, though he did think there was a possibility she might fill him in if she learned anything. But only if it didn't cost her, of course, and only because she would believe that it would cause him to feel like he owed her something.

Which he wouldn't.

"He's gone," Lilah announced on the way back into her bedroom. "You can come out of the closet or from under the bed or wherever you've been hiding."

"I haven't been hiding anywhere," Wesley Wyndam-Pryce objected. "I've been right here."

In fact, he was on top of the bed when she returned, still shirtless, as he had been when she'd left. "Of course," she said. "Because you knew he couldn't enter unless he was invited, and I wasn't likely to invite him. And if I had, you'd still have had time to hide before he reached the bedroom."

"What makes you think I have anything to hide?" he asked. *His English accent,* Lilah thought, *is so cute when he's being defensive.*

"Oh, you've told him about us, then? That we're seeing each other?"

"Angel and I don't really talk about our personal lives anymore." Wesley sounded sorrowful when he said it, as if he and the vamp had once enjoyed locker-room talk together that they could no longer share. Maybe they had. After all, a guy who'd lived as long as Angel would probably have a lot of stories to share, even if Wes was somewhat less experienced.

But she had shown him a few things. More than a few. Tricks he had never known, that had probably never even entered his feeble imagination. She derived great pleasure from corrupting the former Watcher, the good guy gone bad. *Well,* she corrected, *going bad. If I have anything to say about it.*

She climbed onto the bed, drawing one fingernail up Wesley's bare stomach and chest.

And I do, she thought. *I definitely do . . .*

"Hi, Wesley."

Great, Charles Gunn thought. *He walks in and gets a cheerful hello from Fred. I can't even get one of those anymore when she wakes up next to me.* Gunn and Winifred Burkle, who everyone called Fred and with whom he was in love, had been on the outs ever since he had done away with someone who had done her a great wrong.

They all had met Fred when they'd gone to Pylea, Lorne's home dimension, after Cordelia had been accidentally yanked through a dimensional portal. Fred had been sent to Pylea years before, by a college professor she had respected, as it turned out. Once they'd found out who was at fault, Gunn had taken it upon himself to exact the appropriate revenge so Fred wouldn't have to. But instead of being appreciative, Fred had turned frosty, as if frightened by Gunn's cold-blooded initiative. Their budding romance had slammed up against the stone wall of Fred's intransigence, leaving Gunn feeling like he had been blindsided.

And now Wesley—with whom Gunn had been in competition, in the early days after they'd brought her back to L.A., for Fred's affections—had an advantage simply because he hadn't been around when all that had gone down. He was the exotic stranger now, the man on the outside, because of his falling-out with Angel. He got the happy greetings; Gunn got the cold shoulder.

Gunn had long ago given up believing that life should be fair. If he'd had any such illusions, they had ended the day he'd had to dust his own sister because she had become a vampire.

But even though he wasn't looking for fairness, he had at least come to believe that life was once again worth living. Doing good, fighting monsters, being loved by Fred—these things had been like unexpected sunlight after a long storm. Now the storm clouds were back and the days ahead loomed darker than ever.

"Hello, Fred," Wesley replied in that cultured British accent he had. One more way he couldn't compete—Gunn was from the streets, and sounded like it. "Charles."

"Hey, English," Gunn answered. "What's shakin'?"

"I was about to ask the same," Wesley said. Gunn thought he looked a little haggard, like he hadn't been sleeping well or shaving regularly. He was wearing a royal blue silk shirt and nice dark pants, but they were kind of wrinkled, as if he'd been sleeping in them. *Fred probably thinks it's hot. All manly and stuff.* "I hadn't heard from you in a few days, and just wanted to make sure you didn't need me for anything."

"We do, we'll call you," Gunn assured him.

"I think it's very nice of you to check in," Fred added. "Especially considering, you know, everything that's happened. . . ."

"Yes, well," Wesley said. "Water under the bridge, and all that. At least as far as I'm concerned."

Not sure Angel feels the same way, Gunn thought. But the truth was, Angel had stopped making a big issue out of what he saw as Wesley's betrayal. Feelings were still raw between the two longtime comrades, and Gunn wasn't sure they would ever achieve the same level of trust they had once shared. But it was between Angel and Wes. The only remaining hard feelings on Gunn's part had to do with Fred, and the fact that Wes might once again become a rival for her affections.

The way she feels about me right now, he thought, *all he'd have to do is smile right and she'd go home with him.*

"I thought I heard an English accent. Has Hugh Grant finally dropped by to visit, or is that Wesley?" Lorne's voice called from a back office.

"It's Wesley!" Fred shouted back.

"Oh, good," Lorne said, emerging through the office door with a couple of huge books in his hands. Lorne was wearing an open-necked yellow shirt under his luminous blue silk suit, perfectly setting off the bright green of his skin and the red of his lips, eyes, and horns. He was tall, with big hands, but even they seemed dwarfed by the enormous volumes he carried. "I was hoping you'd come around, dumpling," he said. "I've got a couple of questions about these grimoires, and I knew that with your Watcher training you were the guy who could answer them."

"I'll do what I can," Wesley offered. "Which ones are they?"

Before Lorne could answer, the front door opened and Angel walked in. The scowl on his face told everything that needed to be said about his mood. "Fred, Lorne, Wes, Gunn," he said, his voice low, subdued.

"Did you make it to the Fletchers' okay?" Fred asked him.

Angel shot her a fierce glance, but then the anger subsided and was replaced by what looked like sorrowful resignation. "Got there," he said. "But too late."

"Too late as in everyone went to bed already?" Gunn asked with hope.

"Too late as in everyone dead already," Angel replied.

"Oh no, lambchop," Lorne said sympathetically. He put the books down on the hotel's front counter. "How many?"

"Four," Angel said. His tone was flat, but Gunn could see the anguish he felt by his expression. "Two adults, two teens."

"Was the perpetrator still on the premises?" Wesley asked.

"No. I don't know. I didn't see anyone," Angel reported. "But the place felt wrong. So yeah, maybe it was—maybe it just wasn't one that I could see."

"We should go back," Wesley said. "Check it out further."

"We will," Angel said. "I've already checked with a couple of sources, got some informants looking into it. Don't worry about that. Whatever did that to those people, I'll find it. And I'll kill it."

Fred went to Angel and stroked his arm soothingly. "I know you will, Angel," she said. "You always do."

"Maybe," Angel admitted grudgingly. "But I like it better when I'm on time."

"You took off as soon as I took the call, Angel," Lorne reminded him. "It's not like you sat around finishing a poker hand or anything. What else could you have done?"

"I let myself get distracted," Angel told them. "I saw what looked like a vampire attack, and I stopped to prevent it. But then it turned out that the attacker and the victim were both vampires, only not really, and then they both just vanished. Somebody set me up. Someone wanted to slow me down long enough to finish off the Fletchers, and I fell for it."

"But Angel, surely anyone else would have done the same," Wesley said.

"You ever heard of any creatures like that, Wes?" he asked.

"Pose as vampires, and then disappear?"

"Convincing vampires. Not just a shapeshifter or anything. They even smelled right. Then they were gone."

"I'll give it some thought, Angel," Wes promised.

"Remember, big guy," Lorne said. "We didn't know the threat to the Fletchers was real, or urgent. So when you saw something happening right in front of your big brown eyes, you stopped to lend a hand. Nothing wrong with that. You can't beat yourself up over it."

Angel shrugged.

Obviously, Gunn thought, *he's already made up his mind to do just that.*

Three Nights Ago

"I've got a caller on the line. Buck, from Tulsa. What's on your mind tonight, Buck?"

"Am I on?"

"You're on, Buck. This is Mac Lindley."

"Oh, well, howdy, Mac. Longtime listener, first-time caller. Didn't think I'd ever get through."

"Everybody gets through if they've got a little patience, Buck. This is democracy in action. Every voice gets heard."

"That's what's so great about you, Mac. You're not some kind of elitist like some of those other radio people."

"What's your question, Buck?" Mac hated it when listeners went on and on about how great he was. He'd had enough of people's adulation. He'd worked in big markets. He'd opened shopping malls and auto dealerships, appeared at fund-raising events for charities, signed autographs until his hand hurt. No more. These days, almost no one would recognize him when he was out in public. That's the way he liked it.

"Oh well, I was wondering. About those vampires and stuff you were talking about the other night, down there in Los Angeles?"

"What about 'em, Buck?"

"Well, do you think they're working for some foreign government or something? Like the UN, or something like that?"

"I don't know, Buck. I don't think so. But you know, I haven't stopped one and asked him. First thing I'd do if I got my hands on one is drive a stake through his heart, you know? Then if he hung around long enough, I might ask him some questions. But stake first, that's what I'm saying."

"Yeah, Mac, but if they're working for the

enemy, don't you think that's something we ought to know? I mean, maybe the government can do something about it then."

"Buck, Buck, Buck. You sit around and wait for the government to solve your problems, then next thing you know, the vampires and werewolves and such are going to be knocking on your door in the middle of the night. We've got to tend to our own affairs, Buck, that's what I always say. Take care of things ourselves. Government's good for taking our taxes and filling a pothole once in a while. When it comes to something like this, to a danger that threatens the lives of our children, our women, why then, it's up to us to take action. You're never going to get a bunch of senators in Washington to admit that we've got a vampire problem. You're not even likely to get the mayor of Tulsa to requisition crosses and stakes for the local police. No, we don't tend to our own, Buck. No one else is going to help us out."

"I see that, Mac. I get what you're saying. I just—"

"Thanks for calling, Buck from Tulsa. We'll be right back after station identification with more from the Night Country. I'm Mac Lindley, your guide and host here in the darkness."

Joe Ed Hollister gnawed on the end of his wooden toothpick for a moment and then turned to Duane

Pickens and Billy Finn. "You all hear that?" he asked around the chewed-up sliver of wood. They were sitting in his garage, from which he'd banished his pickup in favor of a wet bar and workshop. Currently it was the wet bar getting the most attention, as the three men sat on secondhand barstools enjoying cold brews from the bar's minifridge. The garage was lit by a single overhead bulb, but Joe Ed had also hung white Christmas lights on the wall behind the bar to give it a festive atmosphere. Truth was, he spent more time at the bar than at the workbench, most days. "Monsters right here in the U.S."

"I don't know, Joe Ed," Billy said. Billy was kind of a whiner, Joe Ed had always thought. Even when he wasn't actually complaining, his voice had a nasal twang to it that sounded like a whine, and he drew his words out in a way that annoyed Joe Ed. He put up with the younger man because he would sometimes spring for beer and because Joe Ed's sister Chantal had been married to Billy for about a year, and that made him something like family. "Seems like if they was real vampires we'd've heard about it on the TV news."

"You can't trust the media," Duane declared, as if Mac Lindley weren't the media himself. He had a habit of doing that, just saying what he believed like it was the gospel truth. "Even Fox News is wrong sometimes. If they got some reason they don't want you to know about the vampires, why, then, they're just not gonna tell you about 'em."

"You ever heard of anyone proving Mac Lindley wrong?" Joe Ed asked.

Billy thought on that for a minute. "Can't say as I have. Don't think I ever heard of anyone proving him right, either."

"Exactly!" Duane said, punctuating his outburst by slamming his bottle down on the bar top. Duane was, to put it mildly, a few pounds over the approved weight limit for a man of five ten, and the bottle almost disappeared in his meaty fist. "That's because he's right. The government don't want you to know about that sort of thing, because they know most people want to feel like the government's protecting 'em. So they can't let on that they know about UFOs and bigfoots and vampires and all that stuff." He lowered his voice to a conspiratorial tone. "The very fact that we don't ever hear about it just proves what Mac's been saying all this time."

Listening to them, Joe Ed removed the toothpick from his mouth and examined it as if it were a prized object that should be displayed in a museum somewhere. Then he let his gaze drift over to his friends: Billy—small, dark, and lithe, with a smile that would make an orthodontist dream of tropical vacations, and Duane—who was big and thick from the tips of his sausage-like fingers to the gray buzz cut on his enormous head. Billy wore a George Strait souvenir T-shirt from a concert he hadn't even been to, which he'd picked up secondhand from a thrift store, and Dickies work pants from Sears. Duane's white cowboy shirt didn't quite come together over his belly, which strained the pearl snaps to their limits. Jeans and Frye boots completed his ensemble. "You know," Joe Ed said after a minute, "we should do something about this."

"About what, Joe Ed?" Billy said.

"About vampires and such."

"Do what?" Duane asked.

"Well, that thing you're just about leaning on there is a lathe," Joe Ed pointed out. "We got plenty of wood. Why not make up a bunch of stakes, load our guns, and take us a road trip?"

CHAPTER THREE

Tonight

There were things Lorne would rather have done than go out trying to learn what, if anything, the demonic community knew about the attack on the Fletchers. But since Caritas, his nightclub, had been closed down for the last time, and it didn't look like European travel was in the budget, he figured doing the legwork Angel had asked of him was second best. He owed Angel big-time, anyway, and there wasn't much that Angel could have asked of him that he'd have been unwilling to do.

So here he was, out on a dark L.A. street corner, where he'd just had a brief and unhelpful conversation with a Moolish demon who went by the name of Rat. The demon resembled his name to a disturbing degree, right down to the long, stiff whiskers that protruded from his cheeks, on both sides of a long, pointed nose. Lorne had been pointed Rat's way by a Sontrian who claimed that the Moolish had been talking about casing a house in the hills for some job. But when Lorne talked to him, he learned that the job was in the hills above Pasadena, nowhere near the Fletcher house, and it was a simple robbery meant to occur while the owners were out of town. There was no connection to the Fletchers. Lorne tried to warn Rat not to get involved with it, anyway, just in case, but there was no persuading the young Moolish.

Lorne was about to head back to his car when he heard the sound of wheels screeching around the corner. As always when he was out in the city, exposed to whatever humans were about during the night, he turned away from the street, toward the wall, and tugged the wide brim of his hat down to shield his green skin from view. The car roared past him, and he started to relax.

But before the car reached the far corner, it squealed to a stop in the middle of the street. Lorne swallowed once, certain that the sudden halt was a bad sign. *Time to hit the bricks,* he thought anxiously. *This neighborhood is dangerous enough, even for someone lacking my delicate sensibilities.* He turned back toward the corner, willing to take the long way around to the car he'd parked nearby, if it meant avoiding unnecessary trouble.

He hadn't reached the corner yet when he heard

all four doors of the car that had stopped open and slam shut. Instead of looking back, he broke into a sprint. From behind him, he heard a male voice shout, "There he goes! That's definitely one of them!"

One of what? Lorne wondered as he ran. *Incredibly handsome Pyleans?* Maybe his pursuers were just casting directors looking for a younger, greener George Clooney.

Somehow, he didn't think so. With the sounds of running footsteps echoing through the empty streets, Lorne cranked it up a notch, letting his long legs fly beneath him. He gave up all hope of getting to the car until he had lost these people. His hat caught a breeze and flew from his head, and he didn't stop for it even though it had cost him $39.95 at the Beverly Center. It wasn't so much the money that he regretted, but a green-skinned Pylean didn't get many chances to go shopping at the Beverly Center. He bade it a silent good-bye and kept running.

Hearing traffic on a cross street, Lorne felt hope leap up in him and he redoubled his efforts. His own footsteps sounded almost unbearably loud on the quiet sidewalk, but in another moment the rush of traffic might drown it out. One more corner and he'd be there.

But when he reached the corner and scooted around it, all the cars on the street were off in the distance, red taillights teasing him. He was alone in the night.

Well, not entirely alone.

The noise of pursuit continued, not too far behind him. Lorne could cross the street, or he could continue to run down this side of the block. Neither choice looked especially promising. Darkness in both directions; no place to turn for help.

Where's tall, dark, and fangsome when you really need him? he thought. *Isn't this the time for some knight in shining armor—to scramble a metaphor, because vamps and shining armor rarely mix well—to come dashing to the rescue?*

But if there was any dashing to be done, Lorne would have to do it. More or less at random, he decided to cross the street, and he ran for it, across the empty road. Even the distant taillights were gone now. At least the other side seemed darker, as though the streetlights were more widely spaced— the functioning ones, anyway.

He had barely cleared the street when a backward glance revealed that his pursuers had reached it. He darted into the shadows at the corner, continuing the direction he'd been going instead of down the block, staying close to the wall and trying to run quietly. Those chasing him paused momentarily at the corner, and he guessed they were looking in every direction, trying to guess which way he had gone.

Halfway down the block, he saw the mouth of an alley. Ordinarily Lorne would stay far away from alleys in a neighborhood like this, especially at night. But this was not ordinarily, and he didn't think he had a choice. He turned into the alley.

It was every bit as unpleasant as he'd feared.

It looked like trash collectors had given up coming into the alley, but the locals had continued to toss their garbage there just the same. The stench was almost unbearable—Lorne imagined that, on a sunny day, as opposed to this dark, cool night, it would be enough to make a grown man faint. Or vomit. Maybe both. Passing through the alley would be like wading into an ocean of other people's castoffs.

Breathing through his mouth and hoping he didn't step on anything that squirmed, he forced himself to go in.

The ground was repulsively slick under his feet, and he didn't want to know with what. He tried not to think about it too much, tried to stay focused on the fact that a group of people were chasing him and he didn't know why. But they didn't sound friendly, and in those parts, a demon didn't take his chances. Not if he knew what was good for him, as the old saying went, and Lorne definitely knew what was good for him. Plenty of hydration, lots of sleep, and not being attacked were at the top of the list.

But the farther he got into the alley of disgusting odors, the worse he felt about his decision. The end of the alley was blocked by a tall, chain-link fence. There were a couple of fire escapes along the buildings, but they were the kind that couldn't be reached from the ground unless someone released them from above.

Hell smelled like garbage, and Lorne was trapped there.

"He went this way!" Clayton called. He waved toward the others, Renny and Felipé and Brian, trying to catch their attention. They were still at the corner, unsure of which way the green freak had run, but Clayton had good night vision—his mother had always attributed it to carrots, but he thought DNA had more to do with it—and he was sure the guy had ducked into the alley.

The four of them lived in Huntington Beach, just down the coast in Orange County. When they'd heard Mac Lindley's warnings, it hadn't taken much to persuade one another that they ought to take a drive up to L.A. to see what could be seen. Clayton hadn't really expected to spot anything. Tell the truth, he was pretty sure Mac Lindley was as full of manure as a feed lot, but the man was entertaining to listen to. They had driven around for a couple of hours, getting increasingly more bored and tired, and had been just about ready to head home when Renny had spotted the green guy.

At first, Clayton had been convinced it was just the reflection of neon lights or something. The guy looked human enough, and Clayton was sure no one could have skin of such a bright, emerald green. But the more the other guys shouted about having seen a real monster, the more he thought maybe they were right, which meant that so was Mac Lindley. Felipé had stopped the car and they'd piled out, weapons in hand, but the guy had started running as soon as he'd heard their brakes squeal. Then his hat had blown off and Clayton had seen the horns, and he had known—really *known*—that Lindley was correct: There really were monsters in their midst. He had been running too hard, adrenaline pumping too fast, to know if he was more excited or more scared.

But he felt *something,* he knew. Something more than his usual state of restlessness. Life had become a routine of going to work, eating dinner, having a few drinks with the guys, falling asleep with the radio playing, then getting up and doing it all over again. Even as he lived it, he knew there was something missing—he just hadn't been able to get out of his rut long enough to figure out what. So whatever it was he was experiencing, he liked it. He felt . . . *alive.*

The other guys ran toward him now. Felipé carried a .12 gauge, Renny a baseball bat, Brian a tire iron. Clayton's own weapon was a cleaver from his kitchen. The thought of getting close enough to some kind of otherworldly monster to actually use it filled him with dread, but at the same time with desperate anticipation.

"You see where he went?" Renny asked breathlessly.

"I'm pretty sure he went into that alley," Clayton replied.

"Let's check it out," Felipé urged.

With the comfort of having his buddies close to him, Clayton felt more at ease entering the alley than he had before. It was dark in there, but enough light spilled in to reveal that it was as full of trash as a town dump, and the stench of it almost made him gag. But Renny had a flashlight, which he waved around the alley.

"It's a dead end!" Brian said, excited. "That means he's still in there!"

"If he really went in there in the first place," Renny countered. "Looks pretty gross to me."

"If he's some kinda monster," Brian said, "maybe that's where he lives!"

"Yeah, he's a garbage monster," Felipé added with certainty.

"I didn't come all the way to L.A. to root around in garbage," Renny objected, shooting Clayton a suspicious look. "Especially if we don't know for sure he's in there."

"I saw him," Clayton insisted. "I know he went in there."

"You see him now?" Renny asked. He offered Clayton the flashlight. Clayton wouldn't take it, though. When Renny had shone it around the alley, all he had seen was trash. Accepting the light and looking again would only prove Renny's point.

I did see it, he thought. *I know I did.*

It didn't matter. Renny didn't want to go into the alley, and that was that. Renny would turn all petulant and start to complain if they tried to make him, and then he wouldn't do it, anyway. Clayton looked at the others, but they all understood the same thing about Renny.

"I guess it got away from us," Brian said, sounding disappointed.

"Looks like it," Felipé agreed.

"But at least we know Mac Lindley was right," Clayton pointed out. "There really are monsters here."

"It looks that way," Brian said. "Maybe a good reason to keep out of L.A. awhile."

"You don't want to catch one?" Felipé asked him.

"It isn't that," Brian replied. "I just don't want to get caught by one."

• • •

Lorne waited for five minutes after he heard them leave—*the longest five minutes of my life,* he thought, *if you don't count the ones where they stood around debating whether to get a little dirty.*

There weren't many humans more fastidious than Lorne was, but he was glad that there had been one in that bunch.

The whole affair had been disturbing. They had clearly been prompted to come here by something—apparently by someone named Mac Lindley, whoever that was. They had come armed, and they had come specifically looking for "monsters." While Lorne cringed at that description of himself, he knew that, to humans, he might be considered one. *To ignorant humans, at least,* he amended. *Not to the smart, sophisticated, educated ones with whom I choose to spend my time.*

He rose from underneath the layer of garbage where he'd hidden, trying his best not to inhale. He started to dust his clothes off, but then realized they'd need a lot more than dusting. Burning, most likely.

First he had to get home.

CHAPTER FOUR

Fred had been a mathematician, by profession as well as inclination, and she had always thought of computers as number crunchers that could be handy solving large equations. Before getting trapped in Pylea, she had never used them much for entertainment or research purposes. But after Angel and his friends had brought her back to Earth, she had learned from Cordelia Chase just how easy it was to find out tons of information about almost anything online. She didn't think she was quite at Cordy's level of Internet expertise, but she was trying to get there.

That night, with Cordy not around, Angel had assigned Fred the task of finding out whatever she could about the Fletcher family, while Gunn, Wesley, and Lorne worked the streets to see if there was any information to be had there. Wesley and Gunn had already come back with no luck.

Fred had gone online and employed every trick Cordy had taught her, and a few more that she made up on the spot. After a couple of hours she thought she had amassed a pretty good collection of data, so she jotted down some notes and went looking for Angel. Walking helped; sitting at the computer for so long had made her neck and shoulders stiff. As she wandered through the hotel, she rubbed her shoulders through the soft tan sweater she wore.

She found him in his office, sitting at his desk and poring over a massive leather-bound volume. He glanced up at her. "Hi, Fred," he said distractedly.

"Hi, Angel." She stood there for a few seconds and waited for him to emerge from the book again. When it became clear that he wasn't going to, she cleared her throat. "Umm . . . I found out some stuff. About the Fletchers?"

"That's good," he murmured. Another couple of moments passed, and then her words seemed to sink in. He marked his place with a sheet of notepaper and looked at her. "You did?" He sounded surprised.

"Uh-huh," she said, feeling a swelling of pride at accomplishing something he hadn't expected her to do. Or at least, faster than he had expected. *Cordelia has always been research girl*, she thought, *and he doesn't think of me that way. But since Cordy went away, I've been getting a lot better.*

"What'd you learn?"

She glanced toward a side chair. "Have a seat," he invited.

Fred smiled. "Thank you." Even after so long, she still felt a little shy around Angel, a little hesitant because he was better than her at almost everything. Except when it came to math. At that, she knew, there was almost no one better than her.

She sat down and glanced at her notes and cleared her throat again. "Louise and Herman Fletcher lived on Oak Tree Lane with their two children, Marina, age sixteen, and Paul, age thirteen. Mr. Fletcher was unemployed, though he had previously been a middle manager at a financial services company in Indianola, Iowa. Mrs. Fletcher was employed as a software engineer by Talco Systems in Manhattan Beach. They moved here from Iowa nine months ago, when Louise got the job offer from Talco. Marina went to high school, Paul to middle school. Herman Fletcher had looked for a job but hadn't been able to find anything in his field, and hadn't been willing to settle for anything else."

"You got all that off the Internet?" Angel asked, plainly stunned.

"Well . . . you'd be surprised what you can find out if you can get into someone's e-mail archives,"

Fred admitted. She felt bad about snooping, but figured that since the Fletchers were all dead, they weren't going to object. And maybe it would help Angel find whoever—or whatever—had killed them.

"I bet. Remind me never to archive anything," Angel said.

Nodding her head, she went back to her notes. "They looked to be a pretty typical middle-class American family," she said. "They had plenty of friends back home in Iowa. Not so many here, but they had been there for decades and only here for a few months. I can't find any indication that they had any enemies, and no recorded encounter with the supernatural at all. They felt very lucky to have found the house they did, at such a modest price in a normally very expensive neighborhood. Herman was frustrated at being unable to find a job, but he tried to keep a healthy perspective on it, and meanwhile, Louise was earning enough to make their mortgage payments and keep food on the table."

Angel steepled his fingers and touched his lips with them. "In other words," he said, "there's absolutely no reason whatsoever why some supernatural evil would target them."

"Or any human evil, that I can see."

"Human evil is always the worst kind," Angel said, "because it doesn't necessarily need a reason. The supernatural is almost never random. But I was in the house. It felt . . . wrong, somehow. It didn't feel like a human murder scene. I definitely got a supernatural vibe."

"And then, there's the other thing," Fred said hesitantly, remembering how angry Angel had been about it.

"Right," he agreed, scowling. "The diversion. The two non-vampires who disappeared."

"That definitely points to a supernatural factor," Fred suggested.

Angel nodded. "If it was connected at all."

Fred looked at the ceiling and did some quick calculations in her head. "The chances of it being an unrelated event are 89.3 percent against. I'm rounding down, but it's about that."

"Pretty much what I came up with," Angel said. "Only, without the number part."

Fred was about to say something about how probability was all about numbers and couldn't really be thought about without them, when they heard the front door open and Lorne's voice complaining about something. *Just as well*, Fred thought. *Angel doesn't really like it when I point out things like that*.

She looked at Angel again and saw him wrinkling his nose. "What's that smell?" he asked.

The stench grew more pronounced as Angel headed for the front lobby. Lorne's caterwauling became more pronounced at the same time.

"I'd rather be dunked in a vat of *Brut*," Lorne groused. "I swear, I saw *skunks* running away from me with tears in their eyes!"

"It ain't all that bad," Gunn assured him. But Gunn's voice had a strange, nasal tone to it, and when Angel came out into the lobby, he saw why. Gunn's fingers were holding his nose shut.

"Gunn's . . . ," Wesley began. "Gunn's . . . I'm sorry, Gunn's lying shamelessly. It is every bit as bad as you say, Lorne. And possibly worse."

"I was just tryin' to spare his feelings," Gunn objected.

"Don't bother, precious," Lorne said. His blond hair was disheveled and matted, his camel overcoat stained. Beneath it his bright blue suit was torn and had . . . stuff . . . stuck to it. "Any feelings I might have had are in hibernation until I can remove the top few layers of my skin. And this suit . . . Italian silk. Ruined!"

"What happened, Lorne?" Angel asked.

"Four guys," Lorne said. "They were in a car, but when they saw me, they stopped and started chasing me on foot. I ran, because, you know, self-preservation was one of my New Year's resolutions last year. They kept after me, though, like I was that fake rabbit at a greyhound race. Finally, I ducked into an alley, only it turned out to be an alley where apparently all the trash collectors go to toss stuff that'll make their dump too smelly. And then I discovered that the alley had no other way out."

"And they followed you . . . ," Wesley added.

"That's right. I didn't know what they had in mind, but I don't think it was five friendly hands of Texas Hold 'Em. Especially since one of them was carrying a shotgun."

"So you . . . ," Fred began, but she left the thought unfinished.

"So I burrowed," Lorne said. "I dove under the garbage like Scrooge McDuck in his vault of money. I covered myself up with refuse and stayed put until they gave up and went away."

"I can smell," Angel pointed out.

"Not a lot I could do about that, dumpling," Lorne said. "Halfway here I discovered that I'd somehow wound up with an apple core in my pocket, but even after I tossed that, I still stank to high heaven."

"Those clothes will have to be—"

"I know. Burned," Lorne completed.

"I was going to say sterilized," continued Wesley. "I'm sure burning them would violate about a hundred environmental protection laws."

"I'm glad you're safe, Lorne," Fred said. "That's the important thing." The green demon looked at her and beamed. She did seem to have a knack for saying the right thing, Angel realized. Except for

53

those times when what she said made no sense at all. That didn't happen so much anymore—certainly not like it had when they'd first brought her back from Pylea. Then, she'd been afraid to come out of her room, and what she said was often random and meaningless. He was glad she had finally recovered from her Pylean ordeal.

"I'm going to drain the hot water heater and go through about a dozen loofahs trying to get the smell off me. When I know it's gone and I'm going to survive this catastrophe, then I'll feel safe."

"If I might ask a question," Wesley began. "Not that I hope to delay in any way your disposal and bathing regimen, which I agree is priority one— but, do you have any idea as to why these people were chasing you?"

Lorne pointed a long finger at the ex-Watcher. "Very astute question, Wesley," he said. "From what I could hear, I'm guessing it had something to do with my being green."

"Is that all?" Fred asked. "That's ridiculous. Who doesn't know . . . well, okay, I guess a lot of people don't know anyone who's green—personally, I mean."

"If you don't count Kermit or that frozen vegetable guy," Gunn put in. "But still—these guys were armed. This sounds like they were actively looking for green people. Or for something."

"There was another thing," Lorne added. "A name. Mac Lindley, I think they said. Something about him being right, like spotting me proved some point this Lindley had made."

"You don't know who Mac Lindley is?" Wes asked, sounding amazed.

Angel had never heard the name, either, but Wes seemed so certain that everyone would know it, he didn't ask about it.

"I've never heard of him," Lorne said. "In fact, I try to make a point of not knowing people named Mac, just on general principle."

"You might make an exception in this case," Wesley said. "Mac Lindley is a radio commentator specializing in obscure conspiracy theories, paranormal experiences, alien visitations, and supernatural phenomena."

"That's . . . uhh . . . right," Angel agreed. From the looks on their faces, it was clear that Fred and Gunn hadn't known who the guy was, either, so he didn't feel as bad as he might have.

"So if my presence proved that Mac Lindley was right," Lorne surmised, "then Mac Lindley must have said something on the air about impossibly handsome demons walking the streets of Los Angeles."

"And talented ones too," Fred added.

"But he might not have used those exact words," Gunn suggested.

"Well, there's no accounting for taste, I suppose," Lorne admitted.

"No," Wes agreed. "But if, in fact, Mac Lindley is warning of demons in Los Angeles, it could prove to be a damper on our own activities. Perhaps it's a situation we should look into."

Angel shrugged. "You go ahead, if you want," he said. "If people are coming here to kill demons—present company excepted, of course—then that's just less work for us. Anyway, I've already got my hands full with the Fletcher murders. I let myself get distracted once, and that might have allowed time for their killer to finish the job. I'm not going to let anything divert my attention again until I've got it figured out."

He turned and headed back into the dark comfort of his office. As he went in, he closed the door behind himself.

It didn't block out *all* of the smell, but it helped.

CHAPTER FIVE

Joe Ed had never been to Los Angeles before, and even though he'd seen it plenty on TV shows, the real thing still came as a surprise to him. He had formed an impression of palm trees, Mexican-style buildings with whitewashed walls and red tile roofs, blondes in bikinis all year long, and movie stars in every third car.

The first thing he learned about that was different—different, really, than he could imagine, because there was nothing like it in Odessa, and he'd thought traffic in El Paso was bad—was the congestion on the freeway. They had arrived in L.A. at four thirty on a Friday afternoon, and by six they had traveled less than twenty miles. Joe Ed was behind the wheel of his Dodge Ram truck. His fingers ached from gripping the wheel so hard. His arms and shoulders were as sore as if he'd been lifting weights all afternoon. He was hungry, he was frustrated, and earlier, for about an hour, they had been driving parallel to a skinny blond woman with six acupuncture needles sticking out of her face, and Joe Ed wasn't quite sure if they were in L.A. or had made a wrong turn and ended up on Mars.

"There's an exit up ahead," he muttered. "I'm gonna take it and just get off this road. Maybe there'll be someplace to eat, or a gas station with a store. Something. If I don't get off this freeway, I'm inclined to just leave the truck here and set out walking. By morning we could probably pick it up about ten miles on, still stuck between other folks' bumpers."

"I told you L.A. was like this," Duane said. He had been here before, having brought his kids on a trip to Disneyland and Hollywood before Lenore had gone off to Colorado Springs with them and that aluminum-siding salesman she'd hooked up with. "I told you about the traffic and all."

"Hearin' about it is a whole different thing than experiencing it," Joe Ed shot back. "I've seen pictures of it on TV, too, but you can't really tell on there that the cars aren't moving at all. You can see there's a lot of cars, but you figure they must be goin' somewhere, because if they weren't, they'd call it a parking lot and not a freeway."

Even after they'd escaped the freeway, there

had been traffic and other surprises in store. The buildings weren't all tile-roofed and whitewashed. Stores looked pretty much the same as they did in Odessa or anywhere else. Houses and apartments and office buildings came in a variety of shapes, sizes, and colors, though Joe Ed thought he'd seen more pink houses here in L.A. in one afternoon than there were in all of Texas. There were women who weren't blond, and he didn't see a single one in a bikini. There were trees that weren't palms. And, try as he might, he didn't spot a single movie star, although he thought he recognized someone who'd been in a shampoo commercial once.

Somehow, they managed to find their motel, which was called the Anchor Lodge because the parking lot was dominated by what looked like a rusted-out anchor from an ocean liner, and for which Billy had made reservations on the Internet. They had gone into their room, staked out their beds (Billy would sleep on a foldaway cot, since there were only two doubles in the room), cracked a few beers, and tried to put the effects of the long drive behind them.

After a dinner from a nearby fast-food place, they had returned to the room for brief naps. At eleven, they went out again, this time wearing dark clothes. With Billy, in the backseat of the extended cab, was a leather bag containing a few dozen wooden stakes, a couple of rifles and some boxes of ammo, some crosses, and three bottles of garlic powder—which seemed easier to transport than whole cloves. Mac Lindley had talked about a variety of monsters, but he'd kept coming back to vampires, and his advice on dealing with vampires had seemed a lot more solid and detailed than what he'd had to say about other monsters. Joe Ed figured anything that would take out a vampire would probably put a hurtin' on any other kind of monster, too, so they had decided to pack for vamps and hope for the best.

Joe Ed couldn't help feeling a little nervous about the idea of hunting vampires, but at the same time, he felt a kind of patriotic pride that he was doing his part to keep America safe and bloodsucker-free. He hadn't been old enough to fight in the first Gulf War, but he was too old for the latest one; and anyway, he wasn't sure the army would take him with his trick knee that forecast barometric changes. But he could do his part here, against an enemy that was a lot closer to home, even if he didn't quite consider California part of the United States.

"Where do you reckon we'll find 'em?" Billy asked from the darkness in the truck's cab. Mac Lindley was on the radio, but he was talking about NASA squelching some evidence of life a Martian rover had sent back from the red planet, so Joe Ed didn't mind turning the volume down to hear Billy.

"Vampires, you mean?" Joe Ed responded. The streets were a lot emptier this time of night, for which he was exceedingly grateful.

"Yeah. Where would they hang out?"

"Way Mac tells it, they're on every street corner," Duane said.

"You seen any yet?" Joe Ed asked him.

"I don't know as I have," Duane replied after a moment's consideration. "But maybe. They'd be in disguise, wouldn't they? I mean, they wouldn't be wearin' tuxedos and capes like Dracula or something, right?"

"That's most likely true," Joe Ed admitted. "We got to, I don't know, look for fangs or some such." As he drove, he looked out at the few pedestrians he spotted on the city's nighttime sidewalks. Very few of them had their mouths open, so maybe that wasn't going to work either. "You got your mobile phone, Duane?" he asked. "Why don't you call old Mac and ask him? He's the expert."

"Aw, you know how hard it is to get through to Mac," Duane countered. "I'd be on hold for an hour and my roamin' charges would go through the roof."

"Ain't like you got a wife and kids to spend it on anymore," Billy put in from the back. "Anyhow, you could let me try. I've been on the show before."

They all knew he'd been on before—hardly a

day went by without him recounting the story of his call to Mac Lindley. Joe Ed was surprised he was so proud of it, considering he'd made himself sound like a complete idiot at the time. First, Mac had had to tell him four times to turn his radio down, because with the time lag, Billy couldn't figure out if he should be listening to the Mac on his phone or the one on his radio. When he had that part figured out, he had asked Mac his informed opinion on whether the space shuttle disaster was actually evidence of an extraterrestrial invasion. Mac had told him no, that it most likely was just an accident, though the government was covering up the fact that their own ineptitude had caused it. Billy hadn't let go of the topic so easily—he had heard stories of some kind of electromagnetic burst, which he believed could only have been caused by alien weapons firing upon the shuttle. Mac had finally had to hang up on him.

"I think the problem is all this driving around," Duane opined. "We're not gonna spot a vampire like this. We've got to get out of the truck and mingle with them."

Joe Ed regarded the people he saw on the street. Punks with spiky green hair and leather jackets. Homeless people bundled in overcoats and blankets pushing shopping carts laden with plastic grocery bags. On one corner, a man wearing boxer shorts and no shirt or shoes, but with headphones attached to a tape player he carried in his hand, screamed obscenities to no one in particular. If there was an easy way to tell who was human and who was not, Joe Ed didn't know what it was. But he was pretty sure he didn't want to do any mingling around here.

They compromised. Instead of getting out of the truck, they parked it in a dark area where the streetlights were broken, a district of shuttered storefronts with apartments above them. The reasoning was that there might be some people on the streets—either local residents or stragglers from a late-night club in the area—and therefore bait for hungry vampires. Waiting, they sank down in their seats to make it hard for anyone passing by to spot them inside.

The time passed slowly. In spite of his nap, Joe Ed felt exhausted from the day's long drive, the tension of dealing with L.A. traffic, and the overall excitement of being here with his friends, trying to do their best to stop the threat of vampires from spreading across the land. He yawned and stretched, and at one point he heard a soft snoring from the backseat. He caught Duane's eye. "Billy nodded off."

"Yup."

"Think we should call it a night?"

A pause. "Nope."

Joe Ed considered for a moment, but he

couldn't come up with any reason why they shouldn't. Finally, he asked, "Why not?"

"Vamps most likely don't come out until it's late," Duane explained reasonably. "When there's a lot of folks around, they probably can't do their huntin'. We want to catch one, we're gonna have to be out when they are, and if we want to be a hundred percent sure, we're gonna have to catch one in the act. I don't think we want to be drivin' any wooden stakes into anybody without being pretty doggone certain they're really a vampire."

Joe Ed found himself nodding along. "Makes sense to me," he admitted. They sat a while longer in silence, until Joe Ed caught himself dozing off. Billy's snore had become a steady drone. Joe Ed forced his eyes open and looked over at Duane, who was still upright, eyes open and alert.

"Duane, we got to go back to the motel and get some shut-eye," Joe Ed complained. "I can't stay awake any longer."

Duane rubbed a meaty hand over the gray stubble he called hair. "I thought we came out here to kill some bloodsuckers, but if that's what you want to do, let's do it. But tomorrow let's try to sleep during the day so's we can stay out at night like they do."

"It's a deal," Joe Ed said. He cranked the engine and pressed down on the gas.

The truck's lurching woke Billy. "What's goin' on?"

"We're going back to the motel," Joe Ed explained. "Get some sleep."

"Sounds like a good idea," Billy said. "I could use some sleep."

"You been doing nothin' but sleepin'," Duane countered.

"Well, I'm tired," Billy defended.

Joe Ed didn't want to hear the two argue about it, but he was too sleepy to say anything. He just focused on steering the Dodge truck through the nearly empty streets and trying to find the motel. He'd been driving for about ten minutes when Duane suddenly grabbed his shoulder, almost startling him into driving the truck into a line of parked cars. "What?"

Duane pointed down a shadowy side street. "Over there. I thought I saw something."

"Saw what?" Billy asked. "I didn't see nothing."

"What'd you see, Duane?" Joe Ed asked. He pulled the Dodge to a smooth stop, but cars lined the curb, so he couldn't park it properly.

"I saw someone walking a dog, but then I thought I saw something else, just like a shadow, following along behind them."

"You sure?"

"Sure enough," Duane said. He sounded confident in his judgment. "Let's check it out."

"Grab some stakes out of that bag, Billy," Joe Ed commanded. "And bring the guns."

"Guns won't do nothin' against a vampire," Billy reminded him.

"That's right," Joe Ed agreed. "But we don't know it's a vampire, now, do we?"

Billy chuckled. "Guess that's true," he said. Joe Ed heard a rustling noise as Billy gathered the requested items.

A minute later they were on the street, guns in hand, stakes tucked into their belts for easy access. Duane led them to the side street he'd seen the dog walker turn down. Joe Ed spotted them, too, more than a block away—a man walking a little dog, like a Shih Tzu or something.

And, draped in shadows behind them, another form. As he watched, the other figure got closer and closer, but the man with the dog seemed unaware of its presence.

"I don't know if he's a vampire or just a mugger," Joe Ed said. "But whatever he is, he ain't up to any good. Let's get on down there."

The others murmured their assent, and the three started running. At the sound they made, the dog walker stopped and turned around to see who was running toward him. The vampire—or whatever it was, caught between the three running men and the dog walker—leaped toward the man and dog. Seeing the vampire attack and hearing the scream of the man, Joe Ed tried to urge more speed from his legs. The dog, its leash suddenly released, scampered out into the empty street.

Surprisingly, given his size, Duane edged past Joe Ed and started to put some distance between them. Ahead, the dog walker struggled with his attacker. Joe Ed considered shooting, but the two shapes were too close together—he couldn't be sure he wouldn't hit the victim instead of the assailant.

By the time the three Texans reached them, the struggle was over. The dog walker hung limp in the other one's arms. Joe Ed felt a sick churning in his gut at the sight. Vampire or no, whatever had attacked the guy had dispatched him before they'd been able to interfere. Duane was almost on them, Joe Ed and Billy just a few steps behind, when the assailant dropped its lifeless victim and turned.

Joe Ed was astonished to see that it was a woman. Young—mid-twenties, maybe—with dark hair, wearing a hooded sweatshirt, and jeans with holes in both knees. In the shadows, her raised hood had added height and bulk.

He was more surprised still to see her ridged forehead, long fangs, and the river of blood running down her chin from her interrupted meal. She glared at the newcomers with pinpoint eyes. "Ah, dessert," she said, opening her mouth into what Joe Ed took to be a kind of gruesome smile. He had never been so scared in his life.

Billy charged her first. He took a stake from his

belt and dove at the woman—or vampire, since it was clear now that Mac Lindley had been right that the undead did indeed hunt the night streets of L.A. She sidestepped his attack easily and swatted him as he stumbled past her. He slammed into the concrete wall of a building.

Duane's approach was more cautious. He circled around her, a stake in his fist, occasionally jabbing it at her. She responded by swinging at it. He was probing her, Joe Ed understood, looking for a weakness, a blind spot. But she seemed ready to deal with anything Duane might throw at her.

Which means it's up to me, Joe Ed thought. If Duane could keep her attention riveted on him, then Joe Ed could move in with a sneak attack. It was the only way—the strength she'd already displayed on Billy and her victim was beyond anything the three of them could hope to overcome by themselves. They had to use teamwork, or die right here, at the scene of their first encounter.

He waited until Duane had worked his way around her so that she stood at a three-quarters angle to him. Her gaze was fixed on Duane's stake, watching every tentative thrust it made, only occasionally glancing back in Joe Ed's direction to keep his location fixed in her mind. Duane thrust, retreated, thrust again. And Joe Ed charged, his stake held high, arm out ahead of him and pointed at her chest.

Hands like steel grips clamped down on his forearm and yanked him off-balance. He felt himself
drawn forward until his face was right in the
vamp's. Her breath stank like spoiled meat, and
her eyes were full of hatred. "Think you're pretty
smart, don't you?" she asked. Without waiting for
an answer, she hurled him backward. He rammed
into Duane, felt Duane's stake slice his back, and
hoped his friend had sense enough not to drive it
through his heart. He and Duane fell into the wall,
a tangle of limbs. He dropped his stake in the
effort to maintain his balance.

The vampire watched them, amused by the
whole thing. "Eenie, meenie, minie, moe," she
said, ticking off the three of them with one pointing finger. "Catch some dinner by the toe."

Joe Ed got a grip on his stake again, and he and
Duane tried to extricate themselves from each
other. They had almost gotten untangled when
Billy stood up, still woozy, and pitched forward
against Joe Ed. The impact knocked Joe Ed toward
the vampire. She was intent on their slapstick com-
edy, and knew that Joe Ed was off-balance, merely
falling and not really attacking. She raised an arm
to bat him away from her.

And he saw his one chance.

Instead of catching himself, he allowed his feet
to tangle together, tripping him even more. He fell
faster than the vampire had expected, and so was

able to duck underneath her warding arm. She started to bring the other one up, but Joe Ed shoved his left arm out and she reflexively caught it in her right hand, thereby drawing him close to her again. This time, he was ready.

"You are a clumsy one, aren't you?" she said. He ignored the stink of her breath and brought the stake up with his free right hand, already in so close, she couldn't move to block it in time. Knowing about where her heart should be, he shoved the stake in there and let his forward momentum push it home.

The vampire's eyes widened in surprise and horror as the length of pointed wood sank into her body. Then, a truly startling event occurred. Instead of just collapsing like a dead body would, the vamp exploded into a cloud of black dust. Joe Ed, in the middle of the cloud, clamped his mouth and eyes shut, but he thought he had inhaled some of it, and maybe swallowed some. When he opened his eyes again, the cloud was gone, a few motes remaining on the sidewalk. He spat, trying to clear his mouth of any he might accidentally have sucked in, just in case that would make him turn into a monster too.

But Duane and Billy started laughing and whooping and clapping him on the back, and he forgot about his fears and joined in. "We're pretty good at this, aren't we?" he asked.

"Long as we can fall all over each other, I reckon we can get the job done," Duane answered. "You still want to go to the motel?"

"I think maybe we ought to stay out a while longer," Joe Ed said, revitalized by the combat and the taste of victory, possibly mixed with some of that vampire dust. "Maybe we can kill us one or two more before the sun comes up."

CHAPTER SIX

Night blended inexorably into day, as it had a tendency to do—though, in Angel's memory, there had been a couple of occasions when it had not been that simple. Angel and the others rested for a while, and then continued the investigation in their own ways, each employing his or her special skills. At night, they all gathered back at the Hyperion to update one another on their progress, or lack of it. It was then, with Angel's temper growing ever shorter at the utter paucity of any clues whatsoever, that an unexpected visitor arrived.

Cordelia Chase had once had a tendency to walk into the Hyperion's lobby with a kind of imperious stride as if she owned the place, or owned the people who owned it. That had changed after she had become part demon, then a higher being, then had returned to Earth, apparently restored to human, but with no memory. The whole process had been hard on her. Not that she couldn't recover from it—it would take a lot more than that to put a damper on Cordy's natural high spirits and love of life. But there had definitely been a change, and it showed now in the way she came through the front door the next night—more tentative than before, the whole scale of her entrance somehow smaller, more confined.

She wore a casual, white V-neck top under a black peacoat, with dark pants and pumps, and she walked in quietly, with a tremulous smile to which she didn't seem fully committed. Angel thought that, of everyone in the gang, she had been through more than anyone during the time he'd known her—himself included. And considering he had gone from loving and losing Buffy; moved from Sunnydale to L.A.; joined forces with Doyle; started a detective agency; hooked up with Darla— well, a couple of times, that one—eventually fathering an impossible son with her; had that same son kidnapped by Wesley and taken to a different dimension, where he had grown into his teens in a very short span of Earth-time; and just recently had been confined in a small cage at the bottom of the ocean; that meant he'd been through an awful lot, and Cordelia had endured more.

But looking at her now, he could barely see the teenage terror she had once been, the Queen of

Mean, the princess who had ruled Sunnydale High with a velvet glove and a will of iron. He saw a beautiful, mature woman with whom, he had realized too late, he had fallen in love.

And by the time he was able to tell her that, she couldn't even remember who he was.

Now, he had to satisfy himself with not scaring her away. Any confession of his deeper feelings for her, when she was still getting used to the idea that she was friends with him and his admittedly odd compatriots, might only serve to confuse her, to delay her full recovery. He didn't want that, so he played it cool. Even though she had decided she felt more comfortable staying with his aforementioned son, Connor, than here at the hotel with the rest of them.

"Cordy," Angel said expansively when he saw her. "Hi!"

"Hi, Angel," she said. "Hi Fred, Wes, Gunn." She wrinkled her nose. "What died in here?"

"Does it still smell?" Fred asked. "I guess we've gotten used to it."

"The only casualty was Lorne's pride, thank goodness," Wesley replied.

Cordelia shrugged. "Smells like garbage. And speaking of garbage, can I borrow your vacuum cleaner?"

"Do we have a vacuum cleaner?" Angel asked.

"Of course we do, silly," Fred answered. "It's in the utility closet."

"We have a utility closet?"

"It's like a broom closet, only bigger," Gunn offered.

"So?" Cordy asked. "There's a question on the floor."

"Oh, sure," Angel said, remembering—with some effort—what she had asked. "If we have one, you can borrow it. What do you need a vacuum cleaner for?"

"What does anyone need a vacuum cleaner for?" Cordelia responded. "Vacuuming? Picking up messes of various sorts? You'd be surprised at how bad Connor's housekeeping habits are."

"Maybe if he had ever lived at home for any length of time I could have taught him some," Angel suggested. Then, feeling the looks of every-one else in the room, he relented. "Okay, maybe not my strongest skill. Housekeeping, I mean. And maybe tact. But still, he could have picked up some tips here and there."

"Water under the bridge," Cordelia said. "Or dust under the rug, as it were."

"I guess my real point was," Angel said, now that he'd had a few moments to parse Cordy's request, "why do you need a vacuum cleaner at this hour? It's ten o'clock at night."

She glanced away from him before she answered. "Well, I know you're a vampire, so late hours, right? And . . . oh, okay. I'm not really here for a vacuum cleaner. Although we could use one, so if there's really one to borrow, I'd be happy to take it for a few days. But"—she looked at Angel again, holding his gaze with her big brown eyes— "really, it's Connor."

"What about him?" Angel asked. He was almost afraid to hear the answer. Since the two had grown so close, so quickly, he lived in fear of hearing at some point that she had fallen in love with him— that his son would get to have the kind of relationship with Cordelia that had once seemed within *his* grasp, if only he could have seen it.

But the answer surprised him. "He's missing," she said simply.

"Missing? For how long?" Wesley asked.

"Well, you know Connor. Like father, like son— he doesn't exactly keep a rigid schedule. Usually he goes out at night, patrolling, looking for vampires and whatever. But then he comes home during the day. Today, he never came home. The later it got, the more worried I got. Now, another night is half gone and I still haven't heard anything from him. I'm worried."

"Connor can take care of himself," Angel assured her. It was true. Vampires weren't supposed to be able to have children, and when Darla had become pregnant with Connor, it had been a kind of miracle. The boy had supernatural speed, strength, and ability, although he was not a vampire himself.

"I know he can, Angel," Cordelia replied. "But then, where is he? Why hasn't he come back? I'd feel better if he was just out there with the usual vampires and demons and so on, you know, but from what I hear on the radio, the city's full of amateur monster hunters. What if they saw Connor fighting a vampire and thought he was one too?"

"What monster hunters?" Angel asked. "Are you talking about that guy, what's his name . . . ?"

"Mac Lindley," Wesley said.

"That's right!" Cordelia snapped her fingers. "Connor and I were listening to him a few nights ago and laughing. He's such a stooge. But then Connor said he saw some groups of amateurs in the streets, and Mac was taking calls last night from some who claimed they were here in the city. Connor can handle anything the supernatural world can throw at him. But if he was targeted by humans, he might have a harder time because he wouldn't want to hurt them, and . . ." She looked up at Angel again, eyes glistening with unshed tears. "Can't you just go look for him, Angel? I'm on my knees here. Well, not literally, since I don't want to wreck these Donna Karan pants, but if you vacuumed this floor more often, I might be, just to make a point."

"Point made, applecheeks," Lorne called from the staircase. He came down, still wet from his fourth shower in the last twenty-four hours, wearing a snow-white terry cloth robe and rubbing his head with a yellow towel. "Angel, this confirms what I heard those guys talking about last night, during my short eternity in Hell. This Mac Lindley is, for reasons unknown, stirring up the rubes with talk of monsters loose in the streets of Los Angeles. I was pretty sure those guys I heard earlier were from out of town—maybe not way out of town, but they sounded like they had come here from somewhere else, if you get my drift."

He walked over to Cordelia and embraced her, the only one of the group, Angel realized, who had done so. "You holding up okay, darlin'?" he asked her.

"Sure, you know me," she said. "I mean, I guess you do. I'm fine, I'm just worried about Connor."

"With good reason," Lorne said.

"You don't think Connor can handle a bunch of amateurs?" Angel asked. "Even if they had a reason to go after him, which they wouldn't?"

"I'm just saying it's trouble," Lorne replied. "Remember in *Jaws*, when all those amateur shark hunters went out for the reward? The city's probably a hundred times safer, even with all its demons and vampires, without a bunch of know-nothing would-be Slayers thrown into the mix."

Angel wasn't convinced. "I still think Connor can fend for himself," he said. It was hard for him to prioritize anything over finding his only son, but he knew Connor's skills, knew he was right—second only to himself, probably, Connor was the most self-sufficient being he knew. "He may be busier than usual, if these hunters are stirring things up. Maybe that's why he hasn't come home. I'm sure he's fine, but remember, people, we have real dead bodies to deal with. How do we know that whatever killed the Fletchers doesn't have some other family in its crosshairs right now? I don't want to get distracted from this again."

"Perhaps we can divide our forces," Wesley suggested. "Some of us go out looking for Connor, while the rest focus on the Fletchers."

"And how will we feel when the next family turns up dead because we let our attention slip?" Angel asked.

"Angel," Cordelia said, almost pleading. "You only have one son. I know I don't remember everything yet, but I know how ticked off you were when—sorry to bring this up, Wes—but when Wes took him from you, even though he was only worried about Connor's safety because of some dumb old prophecy. And I know he's a lot more grown up now, he's all rough and tough and everything, and I don't worry about him when he stays out late. But the city is a more dangerous place than usual, and he's never been gone this long, and he is your son. Please . . ."

She may have lost her memory, Angel thought,

but she still knows what buttons to push. It's like manipulation is her superpower. "Okay, Cordy. I'll take a look tonight, and if he's out there, I'll find him. But the rest of you, keep working on the Fletcher thing. Turn over every stone in the city. We need to find out why they were targeted, and by who, and we need to do it fast."

came from sharing secrets with someone he'd never seen.

In this one case, with Crystal, that closeness had led to dates. Dates had led to weekends. Before he knew it she had moved into his place, dumped her own apartment, and was doing his laundry and dishes so he didn't have to. He'd been married twice before, so he knew he wasn't good at it, but he also thought he would recognize the warning signs and get out before things went too far.

Crystal was like a force of nature. She didn't even give him time to catch his breath. Almost before Mac knew her last name, he was head-over-heels in love, flower-buying, poetry-reading, *Friends*-watching in love. It had caught him by surprise, but by then he was so far gone, he believed the surprise was still one more manifestation of the depth of his feelings for her. Crystal helped things along by being blond and blue-eyed, which were two of his weaknesses, with a figure like a pinup girl, which was another one.

She talked him into quitting his job—and he had been in radio long enough to know that a smart man never quits a job; if he wants a change of scenery he'll be fired soon enough—and moving to Cincinnati, where her parents lived. That should have been the clue he needed, but Crystal had just batted those baby blues at him, and he'd made the move.

He had hated Cincinnati ever since.

The only job he'd been able to get there was at a Top 40 station, the kind where he was expected to scream for four hours every day, talk over the beginnings and endings of every song, and generally carry on in a way that made him uncomfortable.

After a year of that, he realized that Crystal was spending more time at the mall with her mother than she did with him. She still batted her eyes and swiveled her hips, but it didn't work on him anymore. Six months later, Crystal was the third ex-Mrs. Lindley.

He realized he was getting caught up in his own private reverie—something that happened more and more these days, as he fell further behind in his sleep. Turning quickly to the microphone, he said, "Listen to this e-mail. It's from listener Marcel, who lives in Alameda—that's up there in the San Francisco Bay Area, for those of you who don't know your West Coast geography. Marcel writes, 'Mac, I'm down here in L.A. with some friends from my hood, and we come down here to kick some monster tail because we heard you talking about it on the radio.' I'm editing a little here, friends, because Marcel's language is a little stronger than the FCC lets us get away with, even here in the Night Country. Anyway, Marcel goes on. 'At first we thought you was buggin', because we didn't see no monsters anywhere. But then on our third night here, we scoped this blue-skinned guy with four eyeballs, standing outside of somebody's crib. We didn't believe our own eyes, then, because none of us ever seen nothing like that before, you know, except on *Creature Features*. But we took a closer look, and it was just like you said. A monster, standing out there plain as day, only at night. We was all strapped, so we started shooting at it, and it went down, and then it kind of burst into flames and burned right up and disappeared.'

"Well, I don't know what you and your friends killed there, Marcel, but I've got to think a blue, four-eyed beast was up to no good. Who knows how many innocent folks that kind of monster might kill in a single day? You've done a service to America, Marcel, and I'm proud and honored that you're a resident of the Night Country.

"Here's another one, listen to this. It's from Barry, who lives in Portland, Oregon. Barry writes, 'Dear Mr. Lindley.' Barry, if you live in the Night Country, you don't have to call me Mister. I'm Mac to my friends, and you're all my friends. But, anyway, Barry says, 'Dear Mr. Lindley. I'm a vegetarian, and I've never fired a gun or hunted a day in my life. I believe animals have just as much right to live on Earth as people do. Maybe more, because they don't destroy their own environment just for financial gain.'

He was on a roll, and he knew it. He could almost see his listeners sitting up in their chairs, or turning up the volume dials in their trucks. He knew there were a lot of long-haul truckers in the Night Country, listening to him while they criss-crossed America delivering vital goods. "Now here I'm thinking, Barry isn't really a resident of the Night Country, because he sounds suspiciously like one of those hippies who's going to start whining about spotted owls or some such, when we've got much more serious problems to deal with in this country than how to save some bird that 99.9 percent of us are never going to see.

"But Mac Lindley is nothing but open-minded, if you've been here with me in the Night Country for long—you know that. So I kept reading. And Barry goes on: 'But when I heard you talking about vampires and other creatures in Los Angeles—unearthly beings, here to kill and ravage and destroy—it just made me furious. I told some of my friends about it, and we got a little group together, even a couple of guys who hunt and have guns. Earth is for Earthlings, and any vampire who drinks blood to live is worse than a serial killer or a big-game trophy hunter, in my book. So I'm writing this from Los Angeles. We haven't seen anything yet, but we're keeping a sharp eye out. We've all got a week off work, and we'll do what we can to keep the world safe for all living things that belong here.'

"Well, Barry, you may be a latte-drinking, Birkenstock-wearing peacenik hippie, but you're okay in my book.

"I tell you, friends, denizens of the Night Country, we need more Americans like Barry and Marcel. They're doing their part, and there're a lot more of you out there in L.A. who are pitching in too. But if you think, truly think, about the geometric progression of vampirism—not to mention werewolves and whatever other kinds of creatures turn their victims into their own kind—then you know we've got a much bigger problem than just a few of our Night Country heroes can cope with. We've got to get out there in force. We've got to arm ourselves to the teeth, and we've got to show no mercy, and we've got to take no prisoners.

"This is important, people. This is vital to the survival of our way of life, of our very lives themselves. Don't let the Marcels and the Barrys among us be the only heroes we've got. Get out there and do your part. I'll do mine—I'll stay on the air as long as some of you are out there fighting for our lives. If you need a hand, give me a call and I'll coordinate activities from right here in Night Country Central. You're out there putting your lives on the line for us, I'll be here for you.

"It's open season on monsters, my friends, and there's enough for everyone."

• • •

Connor stuck to the rooftops.

They'd been on his trail for more than a day. He wasn't exactly sure why. He had been going about his own business—he had, in fact, staged a raid on a nest of vampires he'd been keeping his eye on for several days, waiting until he knew precisely how many were living there and when they'd be in. He had learned that they didn't leave the nest until midnight, so he hit them at nine P.M., when they'd be groggy, just waking up from their day's rest, and still weak with hunger. He had gone into the empty storefront where they dwelled, made short work of the seven vamps inside—taking a few wounds himself, but nothing serious—and then come out again.

And it was outside, when he was wiping blood from his forehead where he'd been nicked by a vampire's claw, that they attacked him.

He counted nine. His first clue that they had targeted him was when an arrow, fired by what seemed to be a skilled bowhunter, pierced his sleeve just as he lowered his arm. He instantly flattened himself on the pavement, dodging a bullet that whistled past where he had been standing a half-second before. Scanning the street, he spotted them—spread out in a semicircle around him, penning him in from every side. They wore combat gear, mostly—camo uniforms, hunting vests, boots—and every one of them was armed to the teeth.

At first, he didn't understand why they were attacking him, or who they were. Rather than contemplate, he swung into action. He could tell at a glance that his attackers were human, not undead, so he didn't want to hurt them if he could avoid it. Instead of going on the offensive, he lurched to his feet, took a couple of zigzagging, running steps, and jumped to the roof of the two-story building. Another arrow arced toward him but fell far short of the mark, the archer surely not expecting him to make such a high leap.

Connor dashed across the flat rooftop and hurled himself over an alley to another building. But the men on the ground followed, tracking his progress even though they couldn't reach his level. They had at least two vehicles between them, plus some kind of organized communication structure, and enough people to nearly match Connor's superhuman stamina. As long as some could rest while others chased, he seemed unable to give them the slip.

Moving across the city, trying to stay ahead of those who tracked him, he realized one possible reason he might have been targeted. His face was caked with blood from his own wounds and the general slaughter in which he'd been engaged. He and Cordy had been listening to Mac Lindley's hysterical reports on the "monster infestation" of Los Angeles, and Connor's assumption was that the people who were after him were part of Mac's listening audience, completely misunderstanding the situation. He would have talked to them if he could have, told them that he was on their side. He tried shouting to them, but every time they had the slightest shot at him, they took it. Engaging them in conversation would have been suicide.

When daylight came, the city awoke, and Connor was sure he'd be able to lose them in the crowds and bustle of city life. They wouldn't keep firing off weapons with people around—he didn't know how the cops hadn't already been called on them, except that as he had traveled around the city during the night, he had seen enough mayhem caused by rank amateurs that he figured official hands were plenty busy.

He really wanted to go home, to get some sleep and check on Cordelia. But as long as they were on his tail, he knew he couldn't—he wouldn't expose her to that kind of danger. Finally, as the afternoon shadows stole over the city, he found an empty apartment in a downtown building and allowed himself a few minutes' rest, just about ten minutes to recharge his batteries. But when he looked outside again, he saw that the nine had grown to thirteen, with another truck.

Connor smacked his palm with his other fist. He didn't have the most even temper in the first place, he knew, but the chase was getting truly

Backup was already on the way. They could hear the distant wail of sirens—probably an EMT unit and one or two more squad cars—as they wound their way up the hill. Julia caught his gaze. "Wait for them, or go in?" she asked.

He had known her long enough to know what her preference would be: She would want to get inside that house. "It's pretty quiet," Ron answered. "Let's check it out." He knew all the arguments against getting involved with one's partner, but when he looked at Julia Mithrow, with her fiery red hair and her plump, full lips and the way her figure filled her uniform, those arguments seemed impossibly vague. She admired courage, preferred a man of action over one who would just sit back and let life happen to him, and that's how Ron wanted to present himself. At a time like this, with a choice between entering a house where, by all odds, there was very little real danger, or standing back and waiting for someone else to arrive, Ron would rather take the initiative than exercise undue caution.

So far, unfortunately, she had shown absolutely no interest in him as anything other than a partner. But she was single and unattached, and they'd only been partners for a couple of months. Ron was willing to take his time, get to know her awhile before he made his move. Ideally, she would realize that he was just the kind of man she wanted, and she'd be the one to move first.

He led the way up to the door and pounded on it with his heavy flashlight. There was no response from within. He pushed the doorbell a couple of times, listening to it chime. Still no answer. Finally, he tried the knob, and it turned in his hand. "It's open," he said, flashing a confident grin at Julia.

He pushed the door wide and stuck his head into the entryway. "LAPD!" he called at the top of his lungs. "Is anyone in here?"

Only silence met his cry. Ron swallowed back some anxiety. It looked like a family house, so the possibility existed that if there was one body inside, there might be more. He made a mental note of having touched the doorknob, which meant his fingerprints would have to be excluded from any found there, and he let his eyes roam over the floor before taking a step inside, careful not to ruin any evidence. A simple footprint tracking blood could be enough to put a killer behind bars, and a careless cop smearing it could set one free. Ron had seventeen years on the job and a good conviction record, partly because he knew when to watch his step. "House is empty," he said to Julia. She was right behind him, passing through the doorway. "The mail carrier said the body he saw was in the living room, right?"

"Well, the pool of blood, anyway," Julia corrected. "The body is still a hypothetical."

Ron nodded. Hypothetical, maybe, but the

raw-meat stink that assailed his nostrils already was as real as could be. He headed through the opening to his left, from where the worst of the smell was emanating.

Entering the living room, he blew out a disgusted sigh. "This place is a real mess, Julia," he said. He clicked off his Maglite, since an overhead chandelier illuminated the charnel house perfectly well. He heard Julia enter behind him and let out a small gasp. He didn't blame her. The state of the room alone—broken furniture, torn wallpaper, signs of a furious struggle—could have elicited such a response, even without the decapitated man in the middle of it all. Fat, bloated flies gorged themselves on the remains. It was all Ron could do to hold in his Noodle House dinner.

He felt a sudden rush of happiness that he was a uniformed cop, and not a crime scene investigator who would have to spend hours in the house with the deceased, or at least with what was left behind once the body was taken away. As a uni, Ron would be in and out in a comparatively short time, and it might be months before he saw another homicide victim. He glanced at Julia. "Let's see if there's anyone else around here," he said. Careful not to step in any blood—though that was a challenge, since it was splattered all over the room—they passed through the living room and searched the rest of the floor.

A staircase led from the kitchen down to a basement workroom, where they found another body. Then they returned to ground level and back to the entryway, where Julia made a horrifying discovery. "Ron," she said, fear causing her voice to tremble. "Wasn't there a door here? Isn't this where we came in?"

"Of course there's a door," he replied. But when he turned to look, he was astonished to see that the door they had come through was invisible—he saw only a featureless white wall where it had been. "It's got to be there somewhere," he said, confused. "Must be hidden somehow."

Julia crossed to the wall, Ron right behind her. They both inspected it up close, feeling its surface with their fingertips, looking for the slightest crack or other sign that the door still existed. But they could find no such evidence, and the wall itself had a strange, repellent feel to it—not so much like a wall of plaster or masonry as like a wall of taut, slightly yielding flesh.

Ron felt a deep, bone-chilling sensation of terror come over him, and for a change, he didn't care if Julia knew it. "I don't like this," he admitted. "I don't like it at all."

CHAPTER EIGHT

Joe Ed and Duane each carried a gasoline can, and Billy covered them with Joe Ed's deer rifle. Joe Ed thought it probably should have been the other way around—Billy could shoot straight up and not even hit sky, whereas lugging a gas can was something he could do without screwing up too badly. But this was just how it happened, and he figured it wouldn't take too long. Making an issue of Billy's firearms incompetence would just have slowed things down all the more.

And all he really wanted was to get done in a hurry.

A caller to the Night Country had identified a particular building, a two-story brick walk-up in the Echo Park neighborhood, as a nest of at least a dozen vampires. This particular caller was a local—someone not willing to take on a dozen bloodsuckers on his own, but more than happy to finger them for someone else. It turned out that Joe Ed and his boys were not far from that vicinity, so they'd had Billy call in—fodder, no doubt, for stories Billy would tell for the rest of his life—and tell Mac that they'd take the nest.

They had wanted to do it in daylight, when the vamps would be sleeping. But once they got there, they discovered that even though the neighborhood was financially strapped, it wasn't empty. Three good old boys in a Dodge truck spreading gasoline all around one particular building would stand out, even in Los Angeles. So they'd had to wait until after dark.

The disadvantage of that, of course, being that after dark, the vampires might well come out to feed. Hence the urgency.

Joe Ed really hadn't come to L.A. to get killed. He'd known it was a possibility, of course. But he had hoped it was a remote one, and he planned to do whatever was in his power to keep it that way. He figured he was more courageous than Billy, but less so than Duane; so as long as he let them set the parameters, he'd be okay.

When it came down to it, he didn't really have all that much to go back to in Odessa. He had been married before, but he wasn't anymore. He had a girl-friend of sorts, a waitress named Lorna he saw a couple of nights a week. She had three kids from a previous marriage, so when he was with them it was kind of like having a ready-made family. But most other nights he either drank with Billy and Duane or sat at home, watching TV or listening to Mac Lindley. Sometimes he went on the computer that Lorna had insisted he buy and studied sports statistics from around the world, which could get interesting. But really, he thought, if he died in L.A., Lorna and the kids would be a little sad about it, but no one else would be too broken up. Chances were, Duane and Billy would die, too, and that would be hard on Chantal, Joe Ed's sister that Billy had married—and if Joe Ed accidentally survived this and Billy didn't, he'd hear about it every day for the rest of his life. And when Joe Ed got himself buried, he figured, she'd show up at the cemetery most days just to continue reaming him out.

Then, of course, he'd be missed at work until they could replace him. He and Billy both detailed cars at a Ford dealership in town, and if neither one came back, they'd be shorthanded for a while. Duane, being "temporarily jobless," as the local papers called it whenever a new bunch of folks were laid off, didn't have much to worry about on that score.

So all in all, it was probably in their best interests, as well as the interests of Odessa Ford and the Ford Motor Company, to make sure they got this over with before the bloodsuckers came out and started feasting on them.

Billy walked close behind Joe Ed as he carried the gas from the truck to the building's base, where he would empty the can. "Joe Ed," Billy said in a whisper. "Once we light this sucker up, how do we know it ain't gonna burn the rest of the block down too?"

Joe Ed unscrewed the cap from the can's nozzle. "I don't reckon we do know that," he said. "But look at it this way. If there's a dozen vampires inside there, how long you think any of their neighbors have to live, anyway? Chances are, most of them have already been turned. And that means their neighbors come next, and so on. Burning this block down is just about the most merciful thing we could do right now."

"What if the guy's wrong?" Billy pressed. "The guy who called up Mac, I mean. What if this ain't a nest?"

"Now, Billy," Duane interjected. "Don't you go worryin' about that. Guy wouldn't have made such a statement if he couldn't back it up. And, anyway, at the very worst, we'd still be sendin' a message loud and clear to all the other vamps and monsters out there. We don't want them in our world, and they got to know it."

"Yeah, I guess that makes sense," Billy said, nodding. "Big fire'll send a right clear message, won't it?"

"That, it will, Billy," Joe Ed agreed. "That it will." He preferred the word "conflagration"—it was a sixty-four-dollar word, but it sounded like what it was. Still, he wasn't going to argue semantics with Billy. "Big fire" served just fine.

The sound of Charles Gunn's footfalls sounded like cannon fire to him in the quiet hallway on the UCLA campus. The brick building had three stories, with ivy covering the outside surface, just like in the college recruiting pamphlets he'd seen. Even though his most recent university experience had been pretty negative, college had always had an appeal for Gunn—it just wasn't something he'd had the chance to follow up on. He suspected that was part of the attraction he felt toward Fred: the knowledge that she was smart and well-educated.

Downstairs there had been big lecture halls, and he wondered what it was like to sit in such a place and soak up the accumulated knowledge of the centuries. Here on the second floor there were only professors' offices, and billboards full of tacked-up notices for tutors and field study opportunities and the like on the walls between the doors. The whole thing seemed kind of enticing and romantic, like a dream of a tropical island paradise. Something he could think about from time to time but would likely never experience for himself.

He was here to meet Dr. Marcus Conrad, a professor with an expertise in Los Angeles history. It had occurred to him that if the Fletchers were as squeaky clean as Fred said they were—and no amount of digging that the rest had done had contradicted that impression—then maybe it was the house they lived in, rather than the family itself, that had attracted whatever force that had done them in. A few questions in that direction had turned up Dr. Conrad, who had written a book about haunted houses in the Los Angeles basin. The general impression was that he was a man who really knew the area's history inside and out, and was also sympathetic to the idea of supernatural phenomena.

He found Dr. Conrad in his office. It was the only door open, and a block of light fell from that door onto the tiled hallway floor. The man himself was immersed in a book, tilted back in a big leather desk chair with his feet up on the desk. He was an African-American man in his early fifties, Gunn guessed, black hair going gray at the temples, dressed in a green loose-fitting silk shirt, buttoned at the neck, and nubby wool pants. The effect was one of unstudied elegance, and Gunn found himself liking the guy right from the start. "Excuse me, Dr. Conrad?"

Dr. Conrad closed the book and looked up at him. "You must be Mr. Gunn."

"That's right. Mind if I come in?"

Dr. Conrad put his feet on the floor and swept an arm toward a guest chair. His office was neat and orderly, with books on the shelves and papers carefully stacked on a credenza. Even a poster advertising a farmworkers' rally with Cesar Chavez, which Gunn judged must have been from the late 1960s, was framed and behind glass. "Make yourself at home," Dr. Conrad said. His voice was low and pleasant. "You said on the phone you had a question about a certain house."

Gunn liked the way he got right to the point, as if he knew there could be lives on the line. "That's right." He gave Dr. Conrad the address. "Do you know anything about it?"

Dr. Conrad scratched his head for a moment. "That address sounds familiar, but I can't place why," he said. Then he smiled. "But the beauty of being an educated man isn't in knowing everything; it's in knowing how to find out what you don't know."

"I'm with you there," Gunn said. "That's exactly why I came to you."

Dr. Conrad turned to his credenza, which Gunn saw had very wide, flat drawers. He opened the third one from the top and slid it out. Inside, Gunn saw the reason for the shape of the drawers—a huge, black-covered book, maybe twenty inches by thirty, lay inside. There weren't a lot of pages in the book, but given its dimensions, Gunn figured that a thicker volume would be unmanageable.

Instead of removing it from the drawer, Dr.

Conrad simply opened the book and paged through it until he found what he was looking for. Gunn could see only lines of words and numbers, and couldn't make out what they signified. Dr. Conrad "hmmed" a couple of times, then jotted something down on a notepad he kept beside his computer. Then he closed the book and slid the drawer closed.

"You get anything?" Gunn asked him.

Dr. Conrad favored him with that smile again. "Patience is a virtue, Mr. Gunn. Addresses can change, over the years, so I just needed to identify precisely where the structure is. Now that I've done that, I can look at the specific history of it." He rose from his desk and crossed to a bookshelf, where there were a dozen or so matching, brown leather-covered volumes, shorter and much thicker than the first book, and went straight to a particular one. He took that off the shelf and carried it to his desk.

"I would have thought you'd use the Internet for this kinda thing," Gunn suggested, a little surprised at the multistep process the professor employed.

"You would think so, wouldn't you? Unfortunately, for as much real value as the Internet has, it is also full of enough misinformation to cloud the minds of every student who has ever walked these hallowed halls. And when it's all presented as gospel truth, it can be hard to know what is real and what isn't. I do use it for certain things—movie showtimes, hotel reservations, and of course I'm on three joke e-mail lists and about a thousand spam lists. But when it comes to serious research, I prefer books."

Gunn was silent as the professor flipped through the pages. After a few minutes, he stopped and read silently to himself. Then he marked his spot with a long, tapered finger and looked seriously at Gunn. "Have you been to this house?" he asked.

"No. Friend of mine was there once."

"I'd recommend he not go back, if at all possible. And I'd recommend that you keep away from it. For that matter, if the decision were mine to make, I'd recommend that the whole property be walled off and never seen again."

"What's the deal?" Gunn asked. He was intrigued by the grim warning. Of course, the guy was a college teacher, so what sounded scary to him wasn't necessarily something that would even raise the eyebrow of someone who fought demons alongside a vampire and had been to another dimension.

Dr. Conrad tapped the surface of his desk a few times. "Let's take it in reverse-chronological order, shall we?"

"Whatever order you want," Gunn said.

"Very well," Dr. Conrad said. The smile was gone now; the professor was all business. "The house that currently occupies that land was only built in nineteen ninety-nine. Most houses in that neighborhood are at least twice as large as that one, and far more expensive. That house was thrown up on the cheap, and in a hurry, so the landowner would have something to unload."

"Why unload?" Gunn asked, becoming curious. Maybe there really was something of note here, after all.

"The house that stood there before was much more of a type like the ones around it," Dr. Conrad replied. "It was built in the nineteen thirties. Three thousand square feet, pool, cabana—the whole Los Angeles hills experience. But of the original owners, one died during construction, and his widow died within two years of taking occupancy. Their adult children inherited the house. Again, early deaths. The place went on the market eventually, and has been both owner-occupied and rented, but no one has ever lived there for more than six or seven years at a time. In nineteen ninety-seven, a new family moved in. They were there for less than a year before a fire burned the structure to the ground, killing them all."

Gunn whistled softly. "Sounds like a hard-luck place to live. You think it's haunted or something?"

"It's worse than that," Dr. Conrad answered. "I told you we would go in reverse chronological order. Well, we've barely gotten started. Before a

This was no way to find someone. It wasn't much of a plan, but it was the best one he had at the moment. Really, he expected that Connor would go home anytime, and when he got there and found Cordy missing, he'd head back to the Hyperion and look for her. So if Angel stayed in that vicinity, he'd find his son sooner or later.

Connor. Cordelia. He loved them both, and yet they both brought him great sadness. Somehow, neither one had been in his life in the way he wanted, for as much time as he'd have preferred. He sometimes thought happiness just wasn't his destiny—that just when he felt drawn to someone who might help him achieve it, that someone was always snatched away, as if Angel's life were plotted out by some cosmic screenwriter with a sadistic streak and a horrible penchant for irony. He had pretty much grown used to the idea that he couldn't be with Buffy, but his time with Cordy had ended before it had really had a chance to begin. And he'd only truly known Connor as an infant—by the time his son had returned from his forced exile, he had grown to distrust his own father. Of course, there was the curse that went along with Angel's having his soul back—that if ever he found perfect happiness, he would once again lose his soul. That put a damper on even hoping for happiness, but he couldn't quite bring himself not to.

Anyway, giving up wasn't in Angel's chemistry. As long as Connor lived, there was hope of reconciliation. A chance that father and son could be together again, a real family. And as long as Cordelia lived, there was the possibility that she would love Angel. Though it would be awkward at first, a household consisting of Angel, Cordy, and Connor might be Angel's best shot at something resembling genuine happiness, even if he didn't trust the real thing. Trouble was, so far he had only a dream, a formless wish. Like looking for Connor—he didn't have a plan. But then, plans weren't his strong suit. Persevering was. He smiled as he ran, thinking about it.

Then he heard the gunfire.

These shots boomed and bounced around the sewers, echoes multiplying them until he didn't know how many were real. It wasn't up on the surface—he was certain it was down here with him.

He ran faster.

Angel was sure the gunfire came from up ahead of him, though the echoes made it difficult to know exactly where. He instantly suspected more of Mac Lindley's misguided followers. The gunfire wasn't constant, but sporadic—a couple of shots, silence, another shot, then a longer silence before a sudden volley of them. Not a pitched firefight like he'd left behind on the surface, then. Maybe a running gun battle.

A few minutes later, the noise of them was deafening, the tunnels becoming thick with acrid smoke that stung his nose and eyes. Then he could see the irregular glow from the muzzle flashes, and he knew he was almost upon them.

He slowed down, walking carefully to avoid making any noise that might be heard during the quiet moments. Not that the people shooting the guns would be able to hear anything—their ears, he suspected, would be ringing for a long time after this. But he wanted to scope the situation before walking into it.

At last, he came around a corner and saw them. Six men, one woman. Definitely Lindley fans—he could tell by the outdoorsy hunting gear, the duck boots, and L.L. Bean jackets. He had come up behind them, and they hurried along the tunnels, in pursuit of their prize.

And without warning, a silhouette emerged at the far end of a tunnel and charged toward them. They reacted as one, raising weapons and opening fire. Angel felt his jaw clench at the sudden racket, his nerves fraying.

Then the silhouetted form was illuminated by their muzzle flashes, still running headlong toward the weapons that spat lead at him, and Angel recognized his own son.

Connor.

Bullets were flying all around him, sparking off

the narrow tunnel walls, shell casings bouncing everywhere. Connor was tough, Angel knew. But his son was also mortal, without a vampire's imperviousness to bullets. A barrage like that would injure Angel, slow him down, but it couldn't kill him. He wasn't sure what it might do to Connor.

And he didn't intend to find out.

He hurtled himself down the sewer tunnel at the hunters. The noise of their own weaponry drowned out the sound of his approach. They were bunched up in the tunnel, their attention riveted on the figure rushing toward them from the other direction, unmindful of the death spraying his way. Angel slammed into the ones at the back, arms spread wide so he'd hit them in a T shape. His forward momentum propelled him into the middle of the group. Gunshots went wild, then fingers fell off triggers as the group tumbled into a pile.

As the hunters realized they were under attack from two directions, they began to fight back. The butt of a rifle smashed against Angel's jaw, whipping his head back. He tried to extricate himself from the mass of writhing humanity, but his feet failed to gain purchase on the slippery sewer floor. Half a dozen hands gripped at his clothes and hair. He lashed out with an elbow, catching someone in the face and feeling bone crunch under the impact. A scream sounded, but compared to the gunfire still ringing in his ears, it seemed muffled and distant.

A secondary impact shuddered the whole group, and Angel knew that his son had joined the fray.

Another rifle came swinging toward Angel, and he caught it in his right hand, yanking it from its owner's grip. But someone else got a hand on it as Angel tugged, and pressed a finger against the trigger. The weapon boomed right in Angel's face, its muzzle flash blindingly bright. He jerked his head to the side and the bullet rushed past, barely grazing his temple. Even so, it stunned him for a moment.

He fell backward, landing face up in the slowly flowing sewage. As if in slow motion, he could see the action unfold before him while he lay there, unable to raise himself. Connor pulled the rifle away from one of the hunters and used it like a club or a baseball bat, swinging for a home run. A couple of them fell under his onslaught, but Angel saw another one lunge toward Connor with a wooden stake in his fist.

Angel tried to cry out, but with the thunder inside his own head, he wasn't sure if his voice was even audible. His fingers pressed against the wet floor, and he managed to force himself partway up, his elbows locking beneath him. But he was too far away to stop the attack. The stake drove into Connor's ribs—too low to hit his heart, Angel knew, which would be fatal even to a human, but damaging nonetheless. Connor screamed in pain, his face

119

contorting, and he gripped the stake and yanked it free. Blood gushed from the wound.

Angel propelled himself to his feet then, still half-blind from the muzzle flash in his eyes but with fierce determination that could not be denied. Like a mindless berserker, he raged against these foolish hunters, these humans who had chosen the wrong target for their insane exercise. He tore into the crowd of them, ignoring the pointed stakes that slashed at him, the weapons aimed at him. Under his furious assault, bones snapped and flesh ripped and blood splashed against dank walls and a floor already invisible beneath a film of murk. He didn't want to kill anyone, but mercy was a secondary consideration at that moment. No one could stand between Angel and his son.

Less than a minute later the tunnel was almost still and silent, except for some moaning and writhing from those Angel had dispatched. He reached Connor, curled in a ball on the foul floor, arms pressed against his wound. Angel knelt in the damp and touched his son's shoulder. "You'll be okay, Connor," he said. "Just hang tough. I'll get you out of here."

"I think you're a little late for the okay part," Connor answered, his voice strained and weak.

Angel rose and hoisted Connor into the air. Connor let out a cry of pain, but Angel held him close, hoping his own bulk could bring the boy comfort, at least on some level. They had never been as attached as Angel thought fathers and sons should be, but still, he believed, there must be some unconscious connection between them. He only knew that he loved his son and wanted him to be safe, to be whole and unbroken.

A quick perusal of the area told him that they were closer to the Hyperion than to the car. Angel took off at a run, cradling Connor in his arms the whole way.

"Things are happening tonight in the Night Country. That's a fact and that's for sure and there's no denying it. You're out there, ladies and gents, taking back the night for those of us who love it. Reclaiming the darkness. Henry and Paul and Stan and Lawrence, Cletus and Joe, Sarah and Sally and Cecelia, Tranh and Bertrille. No matter where you come from, no matter what race, what age, what religion, you've heard old Mac's call to action and you've responded. Los Angeles tonight is a city under siege, a city at war. The humans against the monsters.

"And from all appearances, the humans are winning. We've had reports of vampires staked and exploding into clouds of dust—keep your mouths and noses covered, friends, if you stake a blood-sucker, because we don't know yet what happens if you breathe that in—reports of monsters of various sizes and descriptions, green, red, blue, purple, some with four arms, or nineteen eyes, or wings like a moth, being taken down by loyal denizens of the Night Country.

"Sadly, we've lost some too. Natalie from St. Paul, Nathan from Bakersfield, Artie from Baton Rouge, and others. You just keep calling in, friends, keep old Mac Lindley posted on your victories and your defeats, and I'll stay in this chair and spread the word."

It was losing listeners that was the hardest part. Mac had known that it would happen, of course. And he thought that ultimately, the price paid would be worth the end result.

He realized he had been on this track for a long time, maybe for his whole life. Each job he'd lost or left had pushed him toward the next town, the next gig, the next little piece of the big puzzle that was his life. At each stage, he had learned a little more about the paranormal, had had another experience that had led him in this direction. There had been the time he'd lived in a house that he was certain was haunted, outside Terre Haute. It hadn't been until after he'd moved away from the place and into town—after having been unable to sleep a wink in any of the upstairs bedrooms—that he'd learned that a mass murder had taken place in those same bedrooms.

His second wife, Marie, had claimed to be a bit of a psychic, and after living with her for a while he had found no reason to doubt her. She knew things she shouldn't have had any business knowing. He would go out to lunch with a sponsor and she would know what he had eaten and where, even without soup stains on his shirt to clue her in. She would know secrets without being told, could guess the names and sometimes other personal details of strangers before she met them. When Mac had been ready to divorce her, she had, conveniently, known it even before he'd had a chance to tell her. He'd never had a simpler divorce. But during the time the marriage had lasted, she had been a bottomless source of information about the world of the strange and unexplained, a true student of the occult. She had opened his eyes to many of the world's mysteries.

But probably the most dramatic events, in a lifetime full of them, had been the abductions.

He could never be sure how many of them there had been, because he could never really recall them after the fact. He saw snatches, usually in dreams or in strange and horrific daytime flashbacks (because in those days, he had worked during the day and slept at night). At those times, he had impressions of gray- or green-skinned people with large, bald heads and huge, black, almond-shaped eyes. Their fingers were preternaturally long and narrow, and when they spoke, he heard, or seemed to remember hearing, only a sound like high-pitched dolphin chatter.

He had been living in New Mexico then, in a little town called Madrid, from which he commuted into Santa Fe six mornings a week for a gig on an oldies station. The first thing he noticed was that it was getting harder and harder to get out of bed in the mornings. That had happened before, but it was usually a sign that he was getting sick of his job. In this case, however, he loved the job, and not being able to get up and go to it caused him incredible frustration. But he felt, every morning for a week, like he just wasn't getting any rest at all during the night, even though he couldn't remember having been restless.

And then in the shower one morning, he had noticed the cuts.

He was rubbing soap into his torso when he felt it stinging, and when he examined himself to find out why, he saw a pattern of eight cuts, each two inches long, in a precise star pattern over his right ribcage. He was sure he'd remember having done something like that to himself, and it wasn't the kind of thing that could happen accidentally. It was too neat, too carefully done. He thought about going to a doctor, but instead, he went to an acquaintance, the owner of a psychic bookshop who advertised on the station. Kara Bennett—who very narrowly dodged becoming the fourth Mrs. Lindley—told him that it looked like he was having nocturnal visitors. "From where?" he remembered asking her.

She looked up.

"From the skies," she said, shaking her head. "From the stars."

"Like . . . UFOs?" Mac asked her.

"Exactly like that." She had sat him down and poured him a cup of tea and told him some stories about people she'd known who had been through almost the exact same thing. She explained that the cuts had probably come from where they had done a little biological probing, but also where they had inserted an implant. "You're like a study animal now," she told him. "Like one of those wolves with a tag on its ear."

He was furious at that idea. "How can I get it out?" he wanted to know.

"Why bother?" she asked him. "It won't hurt you, and if it helps them understand us better, then where's the harm?"

Eventually, she had calmed him down. From time to time he had started to remember flashes of what had happened during his abductions. Over the next four years it had happened nine more times—a period of a week, each time. He only knew because of the morning weariness, the odd bits of memory and, each time, the renewed soreness on his side, where the cuts were.

So he had come to this particular sort of radio show naturally, he thought. Or supernaturally. He had given up on things like sponsors, and a salary. He got by on donations from listeners. He lived alone, he broadcast his own show, using a transmitter down in Mexico to dodge the U.S. laws. He wasn't in it for the money anymore, or even for the occasional wife. He was in it because he had finally, at this late stage of his life, discovered that he had a purpose, a message that needed to be delivered.

Most of the time, he was content just to share what he had been through or could learn, and to talk to callers about their experiences. He still wasn't sure where this crusade had come from. For a few days—now that he broadcast all night—he had been sleeping poorly. Bad dreams had plagued his days—not like the old alien dreams, but dark and scary ones, full of unknown monsters he couldn't name, dank rooms with blood flowing across the floors, hooks and chains suspended from the ceilings.

And then one day, a little more than a week ago, he had come out of the dream with a certain knowledge that Los Angeles was under siege from a variety of monsters. With each passing day, he had awakened with more specific information. He had made a few calls, done some online research, and when he felt he had enough information, he had gone public, calling his listeners to their duty.

His listeners were there now—and, more than ever, their lives depended on him. He turned back to the microphone. "I'm told that there's an action in Koreatown where your help is needed, if you've got some weapons and you're not otherwise engaged. A swarm of vampires, the way I hear it, fighting back against some of our Night Country brethren. Olympic Boulevard and Western Avenue, or thereabouts. Get there now if you can—your world is counting on you.

"Ladies and gents, we're not just fighting for ourselves here. We're fighting for everyone. The weak and the strong, the hale and the infirm, those who want for nothing and those who have nothing. If the menace that faces us in the streets of Los Angeles is allowed to break free of the borders of that city, then no place on Earth will be safe. From Afghanistan and Zanzibar, they will come. From Nicaragua and Nigeria, they will arrive. From Peru, from Paris, from Pasadena, they will be summoned. The earth will open to them, and they will issue from its depths. The very crust will split, and they will pass through it. The fissures will part and they will emerge. . . ."

"What the heck is he talking about?" Cordelia asked, a puzzled look on her face. Lorne had brought out a radio and set it up on the counter in the hotel's lobby, and they all sat around listening to Mac Lindley. A TV was on too—its sound turned off, screen showing images of random chaos. The city seemed to be going berserk. Everywhere, buildings were on fire, and looters were taking advantage of the disorder to make off with everything they could put their hands on. Every cop in Los Angeles was on duty, and reinforcements had been called from neighboring cities and the counties of Ventura, Orange, and Riverside. The mayor had been making a statement, but he had sounded so frightened and confused that Cordy had just cranked down the volume.

But Mac Lindley was no better. Fred was just as confused by him as Cordelia was. One moment the man had been making sense—at least as much as he had made since they'd started listening, but that wasn't a lot, she had to admit—but the next, he was off into a bizarre recitation of place names. She didn't get it.

"Yes, it does seem an odd departure, doesn't it?" Wesley said.

"But then, this clown doesn't seem like the sharpest tack in the box in the first place, does he?" Lorne pointed out with a smile. "I'd hesitate to call him crazy, but that's just because I'm so doggoned nice."

"I don't know about crazy," Fred replied. "I

mean, I think maybe I was halfway there myself, back in Pylea."

Wesley broke in with, "Just a little bit, Fred." She knew that was true. She had written on walls—even after being brought back to Los Angeles—long, complex equations. She had shied away from human contact, after the savagery she had experienced there had broken her. She had found it hard to trust, impossible to relax.

She was as close to sane as she had ever been. Angel and his friends were responsible for that, she knew. But she could still remember what it had felt like, then—how her mind had been confused, her own thoughts hard to track, her fears looming larger than anything else. "He doesn't sound crazy to me. Odd, yes. But not crazy."

"Well, peanut, I'll defer to your expertise on this one," Lorne said. "Sounds like a nutjob to me, but that's an uninformed opinion."

"At any rate, he is clearly dangerous," Wesley observed. "He apparently has followers willing to kill, and to die, for him. And doing so, right now. If we could count on them limiting their attentions to vampires, that would be fine. But amateurs aren't always as careful as they might be."

"And besides the chance that they might hurt innocent bystanders," Fred pointed out, "they could also get themselves killed. Do you think there's a way to stop him?"

"It's possible." Wesley rubbed his fingers over his chin. "First we'd have to find out where he broadcasts from, I imagine."

"We could—," Cordelia began, but she stopped mid-sentence. Fred looked up and followed her gaze toward the hotel's front door.

Angel stood there, holding a lifeless body in his arms. The vampire's face looked distraught. Once Fred recognized the body, she understood why.

It was Connor.

CHAPTER TEN

Julia Mithrow had only been with the LAPD for a couple of years. That was long enough, of course, to hear all kinds of war stories from her fellow cops. Most of the time when a shift ended, cops would gather at a local watering hole to talk, drink, and try to get rid of the suspicious, dangerous frame of mind they carried around on the job, before they went home to their families. It was the best opportunity cops had to talk to their own and know they would be understood instead of judged. Naturally, the stories flew fast and furious, each one trying to top the last.

What Julia had not expected was the number of tales she heard that took on some kind of supernatural cast: victims, or suspects, who weren't quite human. Bodies that disappeared. Strange rituals being interrupted. She didn't have the experience to know if it was like that in other cities, other departments, but here, it seemed that almost every cop she met had encountered something that didn't quite fit into her worldview. Sometimes she was convinced they were just making stuff up, that no one could really believe the stories they told. But usually those were the times when the teller seemed most serious, most grim, as if knowing he or she would not be readily believed, but sharing the experience, anyway, because it was easier than carrying it around inside.

None of the stories she had heard could have prepared her for what she had found inside the Fletcher house. The door through which they had entered had simply disappeared. In its place was a wall that looked, and felt, like the underside of something's skin. She prodded at the inside of her own cheek with her tongue, felt the expected bumps and irregularities. That's what the wall was like, only not as wet, and as taut as a drum head.

She and Ron Helvand had run through the house then, checking the windows, the back door they'd seen from the kitchen. But all those things were gone, windows and doors alike. They were trapped in the house, trapped with the dead. She felt panic surge within her. Ron, a little cooler, had tried to radio for help. But the radio hadn't worked either. Julia grabbed a telephone, but there was no dial tone. They were completely cut off from the outside world.

"We'll be okay," Ron assured her. He came toward her, spreading his arms as if to hug her, to comfort her. She knew he wanted her—maybe he thought that was a secret, but it wasn't, not to her—but the feeling was not mutual. He was her partner, and that was all he'd ever be. She didn't find him physically attractive—her tastes tended toward lean, blond, surfer types, and he was dark and greasy and his belt buckle vanished beneath the swell of his gut—and anyway, the last thing she wanted to do was get involved with someone on the job. It was too important to her to risk it just for the sake of fooling around, especially since she had no problem attracting men outside the job. The fact that she didn't have a boyfriend had a lot more to do with a lack of free time—and, she had to admit, with the fact that some guys just had a hard time coping with the idea of a woman who carried a gun and handcuffs every day—than with any lack of prospects.

Normally, she would have just accepted Ron's hug, or waved him off with some teasing remark. Not now—with everything else that was going on, she was in no mood for it. "No, Ron," she said, her voice intentionally glacial. "This is not the time."

He tried to smile, but she saw the hurt in his eyes. She didn't care. He chuckled once and walked past her as if that's what he'd had in mind the whole time. "This is really something, isn't it?" he said. "Have you ever heard of anything like this?"

"Never."

"I can't . . . I can't quite figure it," he said.

She was surprised by his admission—as if he'd expected that he would be able to. Clearly, it wasn't something normal, it wasn't something that might have been covered in the Academy had she only not skipped class that one day. "If you could, I'd think there were some classes I missed at the Academy," she told him.

She thought they had been inside for about twenty minutes, but her watch had stopped, she realized, almost as soon as she'd gone in. There was no place in the house that was comfortable, no place where the smell of violent death couldn't reach them, and, anyway, they didn't want to just sit around. They wanted to get out. They paced and wandered as if the doors or windows might change back again? *Who knows?* she thought. *They just might.*

Ron unholstered his service weapon. "I'm gonna shoot a hole in it," he said. "Then maybe we can call for help. Our backup should be here by now— they're probably right outside, trying to get in."

"Be careful you don't shoot them," Julia warned.

"I'll try not to," he answered. Sweat ran down the sides of his face, and the collar of his uniform shirt was dark with it. "But there's not much I can do about it if they're in the way. We've gotta get out of here."

His hand was visibly shaking as he aimed the gun at the wall. He squeezed off three shots in quick succession. They all bounced off the wall, one of the ricochets coming close enough to Julia that she could feel its hot wind as it passed. "Hey!" she shouted. "That's enough!"

Ron looked sheepish. "I had to try, Julia."

"Yeah," she grumbled. "You tried."

The silence that followed the shots was disturbed by a strange sound. It was kind of a groaning noise, like a house makes when it's settling. But this one was louder than any she had ever heard, loud and long. *The world's biggest creaking door,* she found herself thinking. The image made her shiver. "What was that?"

Ron shrugged. "I would know?"

"I'm just asking for speculation, not certainty," she said.

"Well, I got nothing to speculate. What do you think?"

She shuddered before she even answered the question, and wrapped her arms tightly around herself because the thought that had suddenly entered her consciousness frightened her so. "I think," she said, "you just woke something up."

• • •

"Oh, my God, Connor!" Cordelia shouted. She ran toward them. Angel carried his son's still form to the counter, sidestepping Cordy so she wouldn't slow his progress. Not that Connor was particularly heavy, but he didn't want to carry him any longer than he absolutely had to, worried that to jar him might make his injury worse. "What happened?" she demanded.

"He needs medical attention," Wesley said.

Angel put Connor down on the counter. Connor moaned, but he didn't object when Angel tore his blood-soaked slate-gray shirt away to examine the wound.

"We can take care of him," Cordelia insisted. "I've patched Angel up a million times."

"Just one thing, sugarplum," Lorne put in. "Angel's a vampire. When he's hurt, he gets better fast. But we don't know about Connor."

"I think she's right," Angel said. Connor had lost a lot of blood, much of which had drenched Angel's clothes as he'd carried the young man to the Hyperion, but as he looked at the wound, he saw it wasn't as bad as he'd thought. Maybe the stake hadn't penetrated as far as it had looked like—or maybe Connor healed fast too. "I think we can patch him here."

He felt Wesley's eyes burning into him. Angel knew Wes still felt protective of Connor, and that knowledge continued to tick him off. He didn't bother to turn around and acknowledge the ex-Watcher. "He's my son, Wes," he said flatly. "I wouldn't take the chance if I wasn't sure."

"But how can you be, Angel?" Wesley asked. "He's never—"

"I'll be okay," Connor said with a groan. "No doctors."

Cordelia put a gentle hand on Connor's forehead. "Don't worry," she said reassuringly. "I'll fix you up."

Connor smiled at her. "Okay," he said. His voice was weak, barely audible even at close range.

Fred and Lorne crowded in to clean and dress the wound, and Angel turned away. Everyone was sure they could take care of his son better than he could. *Maybe they're right,* he thought bitterly. *On the other hand, I was the only one who was there tonight when he needed me—the only one who could have helped him then.*

In the quiet moments that followed, he heard the radio blaring: ". . . the battle cry tonight from Thailand to Timbuktu, from Macedonia to Maine . . ."

"What's that idiot doing on?" Angel asked.

"We've been listening to him, hoping to get a sense of what's going on out there," Wesley replied.

"What's going on is that people are listening to him and going nuts," Angel said. His gaze landed on the soundless TV, its screen filled with shifting images of gunfights and explosions. For a moment, a camera rested on a place where a water main had been blown out and shot a stream fifty feet into the air, but then someone had knocked the camera—or the camera operator—over, and the station cut back to its anchors, looking frazzled and lost in the studio. Superimposed behind them was a picture of Mac Lindley. "It's not that complicated."

Wesley disagreed. "I think it's more complex than that, Angel."

Angel wasn't sure how long his limited patience with Wesley would last. "You do, huh? I notice you haven't been out in it."

"I would have been if I'd thought there was anything useful I could have done," Wesley rejoined. "Instead, I've been here, trying to research the situation."

"So the only one with guts enough to go out there himself is Gunn?"

"Hold your horses, Kemo Sabe," Lorne interjected. "It's not a matter of guts. It's a matter of everyone trying to do what they can to figure out what's going on and put a stop to it all. You do remember the Fletchers, right?"

Angel had forgotten them in his worry over Connor. "Of course."

"We've all been working on that situation," Lorne said. "And trying to keep an ear on Rush Limbaugh Junior, there at the same time."

Angel realized he'd overreacted. Between worry over Connor, the whole situation with the Fletchers, and the craziness in the streets, there was just too much going on. He felt like he couldn't get a handle on it, like things were spiraling out of his control. What if he had been too late to help Connor? What if his only son had been killed because of some half-baked radio stunt—or because he had been too preoccupied by the Fletcher situation to go looking for him? He remembered that he'd gone only reluctantly, after Cordelia had insisted. His priority had been the Fletcher murders, not Connor. "Okay," he said, still too angry to apologize, even though he was cooling down by the second. "Okay, I guess we need two fronts."

Angel saw Wes smiling grimly, and thought he knew why. Angel could only wallow in misery for so long before taking action. The fact that Angel was beginning to propose a plan meant that he was back in the saddle. Angel realized he felt the same way himself—as if just by proposing forward momentum, he was pulling himself out of his funk.

"That sounds good, Angel," Lorne said. "Two fronts."

Angel pointed at the radio. "The trouble with this guy is, he has just enough information to be dangerous. Now we know exactly how dangerous. We need to know where he's getting his info, and what his goal is."

"And the other front involves the Fletchers," Wesley suggested.

"That's right. We still need to know what's going on there. If that's what Gunn's working on, then that's good—but if he's found anything out, we need to know."

Angel turned at a sound from behind him, and saw that Connor was now sitting up on the counter, shirtless. Cordelia applied bandages to his wound. Angel turned away.

"Angel!" Fred called excitedly. He walked back to the desk where she sat in front of a glowing computer monitor, catching another unpleasant glimpse of Cordy and Connor on his way.

"What is it, Fred?"

"I've been looking into Mac Lindley's broadcasting operation," she told him, beaming up at him from her chair. "It was Wesley's idea. Lindley's signal is broadcast from below the border, down in Mexico. The broadcasting laws aren't as strict there as they are here, and the signal can be much stronger than U.S. laws would allow."

Angel shrugged. The border was a vast region, stretching from San Diego to Brownsville, Texas. "If we have to cut him off, I guess we can get down there in a few hours. Do we know where in Mexico?"

"Well, that's the thing," Fred said. "It broadcasts from there, but it doesn't originate from there."

She frowned. "Which I guess means it's not very useful information, doesn't it?"

"It's a start." Angel tried to sound more optimistic than he felt. Maybe by the time the sun came up, this would all be over with.

But then again, by the time the sun came up, half of L.A.'s population could be dead. He had thought all along that it was the incident at the Fletcher house that was most urgent, that anything else going on was a distraction. But now the body count seemed to be rising all over the city, and he was no longer quite so certain of his priorities.

"Angel," Wesley said, his voice fraught with concern. "Listen to the radio."

That was the last thing Angel wanted to do, but Wesley's face looked grim as he cocked his own head toward it. Angel joined him.

". . . in the Night Country, with your host, Mac Lindley, coming to you live, from coast to coast, from sea to benighted sea. Tonight, the world trembles. Tonight, the planet quakes. Tonight, it arrives, from beneath our feet it arrives, from beneath our houses it arrives, from beneath our foundations it arrives. The dirt shifts, the soil turns, the ground gives way. From Canada to Canoga Park, you shall feel it. From Fresno to France, you shall hear it. From the Falkland Islands to the Philippines to Fredericksburg, you shall know it."

Angel lost interest quickly. "What about him? He's nuts."

"I don't think so," Wesley said, sounding very serious. "I did think that, at first. But now I think there's something else going on there."

"Like what?"

Wesley tilted his head and looked at the radio, then back at Angel. "The way he repeats certain words, and recites variations on certain phrases. He's been doing that for a few hours now, more and more. Now he's hardly talking at all about what's going on in Los Angeles, and he sounds more deranged than ever. But I think there's an incantatory nature to what he's saying. He's not just droning on like he has been—I believe he's reciting a massive incantation, right now, right there on the radio. And since the city has gone so mad and everyone is tuning in to his station to hear what it's all about—just as we've done, here—that incantation is being beamed from nearly every radio in the city."

"What do you think it's all about?" Angel asked him.

"I have absolutely no idea," Wes replied. "But we need to find out. I'll make some inquiries. One thing I do know: Whatever it is, I'm sure it's not something cheerful."

CHAPTER ELEVEN

Gunn looked at the piece of paper Dr. Conrad had given him, and checked it against the address on the building he stood in front of. They matched. That meant that Edward Revelle, elder of the Gabrielino tribe, lived in one of Compton's worst buildings—a tenement that had been almost completely overrun by gang activity. Nearly every surface was covered with graffiti. Windows were broken out and replaced by sheets of plywood. Doors were made of reinforced steel, with multiple locks. Gunn remembered reading a story in the newspaper about a gang that had kept the grandmother of one of its members imprisoned here for months while they used her apartment as headquarters. Finally, she had managed to escape and had to call the police on her own grandson and his friends. Her grandson had been killed in the ensuing siege.

Gunn shrugged. He had known rich people, and he had known desperately poor ones. In both groups, there were happy and sad, healthy and sick. Having money was fine—he certainly wouldn't turn it down if it was handed to him—but there was no shame in not having it either.

He headed for the door but stopped short when a group of people, laughing and joking among themselves, came around the corner at the end of the block. He could make out weapons in their hands—a couple of crossbows, some stakes, an ax or two. As they passed the circle of illumination from one of the streetlights, Gunn studied them, hoping to determine if they were human or otherwise—and if they were more of Mac Lindley's listeners, would they be able to confine their attention to real monsters, or would they endanger innocents?

But then he recognized a few of them. Chain, Rio, and a couple others of the old gang. Guys he used to run with, used to hunt vamps with back before he'd hooked up with Angel. He thought he had made a step up as far as the company he kept; they considered him a turncoat, hanging with a vampire. They couldn't get it in their heads that Angel was an exception—a vampire, sure, but one dedicated to helping people, redeeming himself by battling his own kind.

Gunn didn't want to talk to the guys, didn't want

to interact with them at all. They'd shown their stripes when they attacked Lorne's karaoke bar, Caritas, which had been a demon sanctuary where demons of every kind interacted together in peace. These guys, Gunn's former friends, couldn't differentiate between that and a vamp nest or a demonic war room of some kind. They didn't deserve two words from Gunn. They were probably having a great time tonight, moving freely, not confined to the shadows, since the authorities had so much other business to attend to. And Gunn was at least fairly confident that they knew enough to just go after demons and leave civilians alone, which was more than he could say about some of the other groups of hunters he'd seen on his way here.

Before they could see him, he pushed through the broken front door and went inside. The floor of the building's entryway was stained and sticky with something dark, and he had a disturbing feeling that it was blood, and not old blood. He tried to ignore it and headed up the dark staircase without touching the banister. Every ten feet or so there was a metal cage that had been intended to protect a lightbulb, but the bulbs had been smashed, anyway.

Edward Revelle's apartment was on the fourth floor. The door had been deeply gouged by what looked like a knife attack, but it almost could have been a bear's claw. Gunn shook his head sadly, and knocked on the door.

The response was a faint voice. "Go away!" it called.

At least that was something. Guy was home, even if he was antisocial. Gunn knocked again. "Mr. Revelle!" he shouted. "My name is Charles Gunn. I was sent by Marcus Conrad. You know him, right? At UCLA? Said he was gonna call you."

A shuffling noise from deep within. When the voice spoke again, it was much closer to the door. "How do I know it's you?"

"Who else would know that?" Gunn asked. "He said you're an elder of the Gabrielinos, and I should ask you about a particular piece of real estate. Up in the hills, in Beverly Glen."

From the other side of the door came a series of rattlings and clickings as various locks were unlocked. Finally, the door opened, just an inch. Inside, Gunn could see an eye, surrounded by deep furrows, looking at him.

"I don't want to talk about that," Edward Revelle said. His voice was still soft, and he wheezed slightly as he spoke.

"Please," Gunn pleaded. "It's very important."

The man opened the door farther. He looked ancient, his face just a mass of wrinkles, his body stooped, bent over almost double. His clothes—a blue shirt with wide windowpane squares, baggy white pants belted tight around his middle—were loose on his tiny frame, and looked as if they'd flutter like a sail in a stiff wind. His hair was white and wispy, combed across the top of his head, where the skin creased and buckled like antique, yellowed parchment.

"Marcus Conrad, eh?" More wheezing.

"That's right, sir," Gunn said.

"Well, then, you'd better come in. Quick, before the rest of the building knows the door's open."

Gunn did as the old man said. As soon as he was inside, Revelle shoved the door closed and went through the whole locking procedure again. When he was finished, he shuffled into his living room, beckoning Gunn the whole way.

"I'm sorry to bother you so late, Mr. Revelle," Gunn said.

"Don't you worry about that," Revelle answered. "I don't sleep much, not anymore. A little, now and then. Never more than an hour at a time. Couple hours a day. Guess I just don't do enough to need a lot of sleep. Not a lot of physical activity, you know?"

The place was small, but clean and neat. The furniture—two chairs, a couch, a coffee table, and a floor lamp—all matched, and looked as if they might have been ordered from a catalogue in 1950. But they were spotless.

Revelle lowered himself into one of the chairs and motioned to Gunn to take the other one. Gunn complied. "You know what place I'm talking about?" he asked. "Up in Beverly Glen? Oak Tree Lane."

"Marcus Conrad called," Revelle told him, nodding. "Used to be the kids, these gangsters around here, they'd cut the phone wires. But now I have one of those mobile phones. No wires. They can't cut it."

"That's good," Gunn said.

"Soon as they make wireless electricity, it'll be good," Revelle replied. "Yes, I know what you're talking about. Marcus told me what place you want to know about. I almost hung up on him. When you knocked, I almost didn't answer at all. I don't like to talk about it."

"Why not?" Gunn asked. "What's it all about?"

Revelle shook his old head wearily. "I've gone for years without talking about it, or even thinking about it," he said. "Decades, maybe. And even if I do . . . even if I tell you everything I know, it won't be enough for you. My information is too little, too . . . I don't know, abbreviated. I don't think I know the whole story."

"Why don't you tell me what you do know?" Gunn suggested. "I wouldn't ask if it wasn't very important, sir. I can promise you that. It might literally be a matter of life and death."

"It always is."

Gunn waited, expectantly, while Revelle gathered his thoughts. The old man cleared his throat a couple of times, and then began. "Revelle don't sound much like an Indian name, does it, son?"

"I was thinkin' that," Gunn replied.

"There's been a lot of interbreeding," Revelle said. "Gabrielinos are mostly all gone. Me and a couple of others, that's about all that's left. The anthropologists leave us alone, probably don't even know we're still here. Think we're extinct, I guess. Well, that's all right with me. If there were a lot of us, that'd be different, but since there's only the couple, and we're all old, why, I'd just as soon they leave us alone. Which they do."

"Yes, sir," Gunn said, just to fill the gap.

"Interviewed my father once, for some study or other. Left me alone . . ." He trailed off, staring at the floor, and for a moment Gunn was afraid he'd fallen asleep. But then he glanced up again, his eyes wide open and as alert as ever. "That land up there, in the hills. Did Marcus tell you about the fire? About the explosion? And the plague?"

"Yes, he did."

"I thought so. Thought he'd be able to find those things in his books. But books only go back so far, right?"

"I suppose so," Gunn admitted.

"That's right," Revelle assured him. "The memory of the Gabrielinos, though, goes back farther than that. Lots farther."

"So you know what was on that land before the

rancho?" Gunn asked. "Something bad happen there?"

"I know what *was* there," Revelle told him. "Grass, and trees. Sometimes birds would land there, or an animal, a coyote or a skunk or a field mouse, would run across it. But often as not, any bird that lit in the tree there would drop to the ground, dead. Often as not, any creature running over the land would falter and stop and keel over. Then when a vulture tried to eat it, or a great condor, it would die too. My people, we built nothing on that land, Mr. Gunn. Nothing at all. That was cursed land. We lived in those hills for ten generations, before the Europeans came to these shores, to those hills. And in all that time, over all those generations, no Gabrielino would have so much as pitched a tent there, much less tried to build on it. We would have nothing to do with that place, nothing at all."

"And then what happened?" Gunn asked him. "After the Europeans?"

"Our people tried to warn them," Revelle said with a sad, wheezing sigh. "But you know Europeans. They don't listen. They never did."

"I hear that," Gunn agreed.

"They built there, and they regretted it. They've been regretting it ever since."

Gunn found himself surprised and fascinated to hear this story. "Why not?" he wondered. "What was the matter with it? How did it get cursed?"

Old Edward Revelle sat back in his chair and touched his fingertips together. "That, Mr. Gunn, is several questions, and the answers are long and complicated. I won't sleep for hours yet, so it doesn't bother me. How much time do you have?"

Angel changed out of his bloody clothes and into a new set—black, like the last. He was not a guy who anguished over what to wear, which he figured probably went along with having more important things on his mind, but maybe also the no-reflection vampire bit.

It was late, now, midnight having been left behind as the planet ground inexorably toward morning. But he couldn't slow down. Too much out there demanded his attention, too many innocent lives might be lost if he didn't do something. It was a huge burden he carried, but he lifted it willingly. He owed it, he thought, to the world for the things he had done. More than that, he was able to fight back against powerful forces, thanks to the combination curse and blessing of his vampiric nature.

He had run up against a stone wall at every turn, investigating the Fletcher family murders. Maybe Gunn was coming up with something, but he didn't answer his cell phone, and Angel couldn't wait around to hear from him. Wes had taken off a few minutes ago, hoping to dig something up about Mac Lindley, and promised to be back within an hour. Angel figured the best thing he could do was to go back to the Fletcher house. That was where the crime had occurred, where whatever had attacked them had been. There had to be some clue, some trace he had overlooked.

The house was a long way off, up in the hills. He'd need wheels. But his car wasn't too far away; if he took the sewers directly there without stopping, he'd make it in twenty minutes, tops. Then another twenty or so on the road and he could be back at the Fletcher place.

He stopped off in the lobby for a moment. The radio remained on, but turned down so it was only a low background drone. Fred was busy working at a computer. Cordelia tended to Connor, who already looked better. Lorne sat in a chair surrounded by big books, flipping anxiously through the pages. They knew what was important—even if they weren't outside fighting the bad guys, they were working on it. They did what they were good at, just like Angel did. The difference was, he was mostly good at punching things, and they had different skills.

He bade them good-bye and set out at a run into a city he feared was bordering on madness.

Wesley lifted his cell phone and dialed a familiar number, but one that he refused to commit to the phone's internal memory. He knew he had to stop seeing Lilah Morgan. The whole thing made no sense to him, when he allowed himself to really think about it. He had no illusions about the nature of their relationship—he fulfilled some strange need in her, but she did not love him.

And the same in reverse. He couldn't have put a name to why he continued to be drawn to her, but he knew it wasn't healthy or wise, and he couldn't let it go on.

Perhaps his father had ruined his chances of having a healthy relationship. Perhaps if one started life in a twisted, emotionally strangled family, one was doomed to repeat it. He liked to believe that wasn't the case, that he could have a satisfying emotional life. So far, though, that was only a theory with no concrete evidence to back it up.

"What is it?" Lilah asked when she answered the phone. She had caller ID, so she knew who it was before she picked up. She had been asleep; her voice was thick and husky.

"Lilah, I need a favor," Wesley said.

"You had your favor earlier this evening," she reminded him cruelly. "A couple of them, as I recall. Then you ran out on me right after goody two-shoes left. What makes you think I owe you anything?"

"I never said you did," Wesley answered. He sat in a parked car, a few blocks from the Hyperion

Hotel; he hadn't wanted anyone at the hotel to know who he was calling. "I'm only asking."

"What is it?" Lilah demanded.

"Mac Lindley. The radio commentator. I need to know what you know about him. Or, more precisely, what Wolfram and Hart knows about him."

A long pause. "Obviously, we're paying attention now," she said finally. "There have been a couple of meetings about him this week. Until recently, he's been considered just a flake, a nutcase. We leak to him once in a while when we want some cover story to get out to the crackpot community. That's about it."

"So you don't know where he got his information about vampires and other monsters in Los Angeles?" Wesley pressed. "Or what his agenda is in revealing it now?"

"Not a clue," Lilah replied, stifling a yawn. "Is that it? Because I have an early day tomorrow, which I think you knew."

"One more thing," he said. "Do you have any idea how I might learn more about him? Anyone who knows him better than you do?"

Lilah considered for a moment before she answered. "There's a guy named Merv Willoughby," she said. "Used to be on the air with Lindley at one of his first radio jobs. He's the one we use now when we need to pass something on to Lindley without him knowing where it came from."

"Fine," Wesley said. "How can I get in touch with him?"

"You could try calling him," Lilah suggested. "He's on the air now. He's got a midnight-to-six call-in show."

Instead, Wesley talked Lilah into making the phone call herself, which she grudgingly agreed to. The radio station from which Merv Willoughby broadcast was in a nine-story building where Hollywood blended into West Hollywood, only a few miles away. Of course, on this particular night, a few miles could take a long time to traverse, and Wesley was mindful of the promise he'd made the others about not being gone long. He had a sense that things would get worse before they got better, and when they got really bad, he wanted to be there to lend his hand to the battle.

He did appreciate Lilah's assistance. She could do that sometimes, be surprisingly helpful when it would be mutually beneficial. This time, if there was an angle for her in it—and there usually was— he couldn't see what it might be. Probably it would just be a favor she would call in on some future occasion.

Wesley negotiated the dark Hollywood streets, dodging emergency vehicles and the occasional military transport, and a few minutes later he was at the door of KJWR-AM. A pudgy uniformed security guard buzzed him in.

"My name is Wesley Wyndam-Pryce," he said. "Merv Willoughby is expecting me."

The guard scanned a clipboard as if there were lots of visitors whose names had to be checked. But the little waiting area was empty, and the guard looked sleepy. A voice emanated from hidden speakers, but the volume was turned down too low to really hear. Wes wondered if there was anyone listening to Willoughby tonight, or if all the radios were tuned into Mac Lindley.

"Okay, gotcha," the guard said after a moment. "I'll walk you back. He's on the air, so don't talk unless he gives you the okay sign."

"Right, of course," Wesley said.

The guard led him down a darkened corridor. Above one door, a red light burned. "In there," the guard said. "Red light means he's on air."

"I understand," Wesley agreed. The guard opened the door and ushered Wesley inside. Merv Willoughby sat in a soundproofed, enclosed booth, a room of its own inside the larger room. He pointed a finger at Wesley, and then beckoned. The guard nodded once and left, and Wesley let himself into the broadcast booth. Merv pressed a finger over his lips. He wore earphones, but the male voice that spoke to him was audible without them. Merv gestured toward a leather guest chair, and Wesley sat down.

". . . government just can't be trusted," the voice

said, somewhat breathlessly. "I don't want them choosing how to spend my tax money."

"So you're a self-made millionaire," Merv countered. "Never made a wrong financial decision. Never paid for something with a credit card because you couldn't raise the cash?"

"That's not what I'm saying," the voice protested. "I just don't think my taxes should—"

"Let me break in here," Merv interrupted. "You drive on public roads? Did you go to public schools, and do your kids? If your house is on fire, do you expect the fire department to come and put it out? Los Angeles is a mess tonight, and we've got police and National Guard and all kinds of emergency services out there trying to calm things down. Taxes, my friend, are part of the price we pay for living in this country, and while it's fine to disagree over who pays how much and what the nation's overriding goals are, it's not okay to just say, I don't feel like paying any taxes even though everybody else does, because I want to keep every penny I can."

Merv clicked off the caller's connection and punched another button, starting a commercial. He turned to Wesley. "Sometimes I get sick of my own fans," he said. "That's probably a bad thing to say, isn't it? At least to a stranger."

"I completely understand," Wesley assured him.

"Anyway, Lilah said you wanted to talk about

Mac. We have to go fast, since I can only talk during the ad breaks."

"Very well," Wesley said. "I just want to find out if you know why he would suddenly be engaged in what seems like a very odd pursuit. I am, frankly, a bit worried about him."

"You and me both, Mr.—Pryce?"

"Wyndam-Pryce."

"Right. Well, I gotta tell you, Mac always was one of the strangest fish in the aquarium, even going back to our days together in Pittsburgh. . . ."

Caleb and Dan were old friends. They'd grown up near each other in the Bitterroot region of Montana, hunting and fishing in the Rocky Mountains, living what they still considered a near-idyllic life. As the years passed, things had changed for both of them—Caleb found that a facility with numbers led to a career as an accountant, while Dan remained an outdoorsman of a sort, working as a geologist for an oil company. Twice a year, they made time to get together for some activity—often as not, a hunting or fishing trip to the few of their childhood haunts that hadn't been paved, harvested, or developed out of existence.

This year, thanks to Mac Lindley, the trip was to Los Angeles instead.

Dan didn't think of himself as any kind of hero, and he doubted that Caleb did. They were just regular guys who lived ordinary lives. They watched TV and shopped at supermarkets and married women with whom they had fallen in love. Dan had two kids, Caleb none. Dan loved country music and Disneyland, Caleb leaned toward classic rock and Las Vegas.

But they both loved America and had reasons, they believed, for wanting to protect their country. When Mac Lindley had spoken so convincingly of the threat from monsters in Los Angeles, both had agreed that they needed to do something. Maybe, Caleb had said, all those childhood hunting trips were meant as preparation for this one event.

So they had come to Los Angeles in Dan's Jeep, following Interstate 5 through the night and day—Caleb lived in Missoula, and Dan in Spokane, Washington—taking turns behind the wheel and sleeping. They arrived late; Mac Lindley was already telling stories of listeners who had called in with success stories, others of tragedies. The action had begun without them.

But there were still plenty of monsters to kill, they reasoned. Until all the monsters had fallen, there would be a need for them and their weapons. They listened to Mac on the radio and consulted a map of the city that they'd purchased at a gas station in Santa Clarita and tried to determine where they would be of the most use.

What they found resembled a war zone more

than a city. Helicopters rumbled through dark skies, shining spotlights down as if tethered by them to the earth. Sirens cut the night, and everywhere they saw the flashing lights of emergency vehicles. Mac Lindley reported that the governor had called out the National Guard, and as they traveled the city's streets they saw olive green trucks and uniformed soldiers, as well as police in full riot gear with helmets and shields.

Caleb turned to Dan, who drove, and smiled. Caleb didn't look like an accountant—he was a big bear of a man, with thick red hair and a Grizzly Adams beard, and hair curling up out of the open neck of his plaid shirt. Dan, on the other hand, was lean and precise—even his canvas, many-pocketed pants had carefully ironed creases. "Looks like old Mac has got a powerful reach with that radio show, doesn't it?"

Dan nodded grimly. This wasn't quite what he'd been expecting. In truth, he couldn't explain what he had thought they'd find here, but it wasn't this. This was serious business. People had died here, and more doubtless would. He was shaken by a sudden conviction that he'd be one of them—that, having entered L.A. during this crisis, he wouldn't be leaving except in a coffin.

Caleb held the map open in his lap. "Santa Monica is toward the west, toward the water," he said. Mac had reported a few minutes before about a standoff in a Santa Monica arts complex called Bergamot Station, where some listeners had surrounded what they claimed was a tribe of horned purple demons. Caleb had determined that they were closer to that than to any of the other hot spots they'd heard about. "Make a right at the next intersection."

"Got it," Dan said. The sound of an explosion not too far away unnerved him, and he nearly sideswiped a car passing by in the other direction. But he regained control of the Jeep and made the turn Caleb had indicated. "Caleb?" he said after a few silent moments.

"Yeah?"

"You think maybe this was a mistake? That we shouldn't have come here? Maybe we're, I don't know, out of our league?"

He felt Caleb's gaze burning into him. "Not at all," Caleb said firmly. "You want to let me out here, you just say the word and you can drive away. But I'm going to kill some monsters before I go home."

Dan clutched the wheel more firmly because he suddenly felt a shudder that threatened to make his hands bounce around on it. "No, I'm with you," he declared. "Just wanted to make sure you felt the same way."

Caleb seemed like he was about to say something else when a sudden urgency in Mac Lindley's voice captured his attention. He turned the radio up.

". . . got a situation building in Echo Park," Lindley said. "This is an all-hands-on-deck emergency, the way I hear it. If you're not actively involved in something right now, your fellow denizens of the Night Country would appreciate your immediate assistance at the corner of Kensington and Crosby. From the pits it will come, from the ruins it will arrive, from the . . ."

Caleb turned the radio back down. Dan had begun to seriously worry about Mac Lindley since he'd started that nonsense talk earlier in the night. He'd been on the air pretty steadily, and maybe he was just growing exhausted. But still, it sounded pretty crazy.

"Turn right," Caleb directed. "We can catch Santa Monica Boulevard back to the 101 and make Echo Park in no time."

Dan did as he was told. The monster hunters at Bergamot Station were on their own, he figured. Well, that was okay with him. The longer they drove around looking for the action, the less likely they were to find any.

CHAPTER TWELVE

"I got it!" Fred shouted triumphantly. She instantly felt embarrassed for her outburst, but she couldn't disguise the smile on her face.

"Got what, pumpkin?" Lorne asked from his chair.

"I traced Mac Lindley's broadcast signal from the tower in Mexico back to where it originates."

"You can do that on the Internet?" Wesley asked, sounding surprised. He had just come back in a couple of minutes before, and had been about to describe what he had learned about Lindley when she had interrupted.

"If you know what you're doing," Fred said. Always a believer in credit where it was due, she added, "Which I do, thanks to some tricks Cordelia taught me."

Cordy beamed. "I do what I can."

"You do great," Connor said. He performed a couple of quick spin-kicks and a leap. "I feel fine. You're not only a computer whiz, you're a healer."

"I put a bandage on you," Cordelia protested. "You did the rest."

"Not that you're not a true wonder of the world, darlin'," Lorne put in, "but I think we should get back to what Fred learned. Where does the signal come from?"

"Well," Fred said. She dialed a phone, listened for a moment. "It's not too far away. In Norco. I got a phone number, too, but no one seems to be answering." After another few rings, she hung up.

Norco was on the other side of the Riverside County line. Probably an hour away, in normal traffic. Which, given that this was L.A., was a meaningless phrase, when traffic could jam up on a major freeway at three in the morning for no visible reason. Tonight, she guessed, given everything that was going on outside—at least, according to the various reports she'd heard from Angel and Mac Lindley, and the sheer number of sirens and other frightening noises they could hear from inside the hotel—was not likely to be "normal" at all.

"Perhaps we should pay him a visit, then," Wesley suggested. "Try to put an end to his broadcast before he gets more innocents killed. On the way, I can tell you what I've learned about him."

"I'm all for free speech and freedom of the press," Lorne interjected. "But this guy is effectively running around to every crowded theater in the twenty-plex and shouting, 'Fire.' He needs to be stopped."

Fred jotted down the address she had come up with on a piece of paper, and was about to stand when the phone that she had been using a moment before rang, startling her. She was nearest to it, so she grabbed the handset and answered.

"Hey, Fred." It was Charles. Conflicting emotions warred within her at the sound of his voice. Once, not so long ago, she would have warmed just to hear it. But now . . . now it just made her uncomfortable. He still loved her, she knew. She just wasn't so sure she seconded the emotion.

"Hi, Charles."

"Is Angel there?"

"No," she replied. "He's on his way back to the Fletcher house."

"Can you get a message to him? I've been callin' him, but cell signals are a little iffy tonight—I think maybe some of the booster stations have been knocked down or something. I've been tryin' for twenty minutes just to get through to you, and don't know how long I've got before it cuts out again."

"Okay," Fred said. "What is it?"

"I tracked down some info about the land the

Fletcher house stands on. It's kind of creepy, in a ridiculous sort of way, but I think it might be important."

Fred still had the pen in her hand and the notepad on the desk. "I'm ready, Charles."

"Okay, here's what I got. The land itself has been cursed for centuries—or at least that's what this old Native American guy tells me. His people were here for generations before the white people ever came, but he says it goes back even farther than that—back to stories he says his people were told by the descendants of the people who lived in the area long before them. These stories have been handed down orally. No one has ever written them down because they're too scared that might wake them up."

"Wake who up?" Fred asked. "You're losing me, Charles."

"Yeah, sorry. I'm still tryin' to figure it all out in my own head. Basically, here it is the way this guy told it to me. In the way back times, these stories say, Earth was a battleground—and sometimes a haven, a place of refuge—for incredibly powerful beings. The stories told about these beings eventually were recited as the myths of ancient people, all over the world, and the beings were described in some of these myths as 'gods.' Sometimes they were called 'devils,' though, or other names.

"According to this one story, two of these gods

lived on a hillside near the sea. They were deeply in love and were never seen separated from each other. The female was incredibly beautiful, and from her all the beauty of the hills and valleys and the seashore sprang.

"But there was another god, a malevolent, nasty one, and he was jealous of all this beauty and the love these two shared. He worked and he worked and finally he came up with a way to get rid of the male god, whom he saw as a rival for the female's attention." Gunn chuckled. "I guess he didn't figure maybe he needed to have something in common with her too. Anyway, he succeeded in banishing the male to the center of the earth. Only a specific incantation could return the male to the surface, where his girlfriend lived.

"But the bad guy didn't play his cards quite right. Instead of going, 'Oh, he's gone, I'll just shack up with the evil god that sent him packin',' the goddess was heartbroken and she hid herself away, vowing to return only when her one true love did. But until he returned, she would make sure that the path was clear for him. The theory is, the ground where the Fletcher house stands is the place he's supposed to return to. Nothing that's ever been built there has lasted for long, and this guy says that's because the goddess's magick keeps trying to clear the way in case her fella can come back."

Charles fell silent, so Fred guessed his story was over. "That's interesting," she said. "But I don't see how it helps."

"I don't either," Charles admitted. "But I thought Angel should know. Just in case it means more to him than it does to us."

"Okay, Charles, I'll try to tell him. Are you coming back here?"

"I'm tryin'," he said. "The roads aren't exactly clear, and there's fools with guns all over the place tying things up. I'll be there as soon as I can."

"We may not be here when you get in," she told him. She described what she'd found out about the broadcast originating in Norco. "I think we're heading down there to try to get him to go off the air."

"You be careful, Fred. We don't know a lot about what's goin' on tonight, but it ain't good. That much is for sure."

"I'll be with Wesley and Lorne and Connor and Cordelia," she assured him. "Nothing's going to happen to me."

"Just be careful."

When he had disconnected, she tried Angel's cell phone. He answered on the second ring, and she described what Charles had told her, consulting her notes to make sure she didn't miss any details. When she was finished, Angel thanked her.

"I don't know what it means either," he said.

"But it's probably better to know than not to know."

Fred agreed, and told him about Norco, and Wesley's idea that they go there for a visit.

"Good idea," Angel said. "The sooner you can pull the plug on that clown, the better it'll be for all of us."

"That's what we thought too," she said. "We're on the way, then. Charles is trying to get back here to the hotel."

"He'll probably have a hard time—a lot of the streets are almost impassable. I'm not making very good time either."

"We'll do what we can, Angel," Fred said.

"You always do, Fred. Be careful. I'll see you later."

She hung up the phone. "Looks like the boss wants us to take a road trip."

Angel tossed his phone onto the passenger seat. Getting to his car had been no problem, since he took the sewer route. But from that point it had been slow going. He had made his way through city streets to the 101, heading north, figuring that freeways would be less impacted by the night's insanity than regular streets.

But that turned out to be wishful thinking.

The freeway was jammed, bumper to bumper. He crawled along, never getting to more than fifteen or twenty miles an hour. *At least it's moving,* he told himself. *However slow, it's better than being at a dead stop down on a gridlocked surface street.*

As he passed Echo Park, on his right, Angel saw flames leaping from a block of apartment buildings. More fallout from Mac Lindley and his fans, he figured, remembering that the word "fan" originally came from "fanatic." He steeled himself—there was too much destruction around for him to do anything about all of it—for devastation everywhere he looked.

But then as he drove slowly past the buildings, he saw people in upstairs apartments, waving their arms frantically, desperate for assistance. Flames licked at the walls just beneath them. Angel guessed there were just too many fires in the city for emergency services to cope with. Those people would die if something wasn't done.

Another stupid distraction. He cursed himself for being unable to look away. But he knew if he just drove on, those screams would echo in his memory forever. He couldn't get off the freeway for at least another mile or so, in the car, and at the speed he was crawling, that might be too late. Instead of waiting, he pulled off the freeway onto the narrow shoulder and abandoned the GTX, jumping down to ground level.

A chain-link fence separated the freeway from

the residential neighborhood that faced onto it. Angel found a break in it and slipped through, then dashed up a scrubby hillside toward the flaming building. The heat hit him as he approached it, as solid as a wall. He forced himself through it. Here, the fire roared; bits of the building drifted past, the flames tearing them free and making them lighter than air. Angel batted flying cinders aside.

From here, he could see that the entire block was engulfed. Flames shot up the outside of the walls, licking out of broken windows. People on the first and second floors had probably been able to escape, he guessed, but those on the third floor risked breaking legs—or necks—if they jumped from that height. Anyone who lived that high up should have an emergency fire ladder, Angel knew, but not everyone followed that basic rule. And this was not the wealthiest of neighborhoods, which meant that simply putting food on the table probably took precedence over purchases like that.

He worked his way around to the front of the nearest building. People stood back, watching from beyond the ring of the worst heat, and one enterprising woman had trained a garden hose on the building. At Angel's request, she sprayed him down while he tried to figure out the best approach.

The staircase was internal, not external as he had

hoped. The front door was clogged with flame, but there was no way in that wasn't. He took a final breath of the relatively cool outside air and dove through the entrance, feeling the heat sear his skin. He landed inside, and ran immediately up a staircase that wound up the building, encircling a central elevator shaft. The fire had already raced through here; the steps creaked and groaned beneath him, but he ran up so fast, stepping so lightly that by the time his weight settled on one stair, some of it was already distributed onto a higher one. They all held.

At the top of the staircase was a hallway with flames running its length, floor to ceiling. The air was thick with smoke. Doors were closed along it, and Angel, having seen the residents at their windows calling for help, knew that the people in these apartments had done the sensible thing and kept their doors closed against the fire. But that didn't do them any good now, because salvation wouldn't come from the windows.

No time for niceties. He kicked through the first of the doors. Inside, a mother with two children huddled near the window with a wet blanket held before them. All three coughed in the smoke, and Angel knew they'd be suffering from smoke inhalation if they stayed in the room any longer. Angel tried to smile comfortingly, then gave that up and just snatched the kids, lifting one to each shoulder.

"You'll be fine!" he shouted over the thunder and snap of the fire. The kids, both under seven, began to bawl. Angel ignored their tears and turned to the mother. "I'll be right back for you," he promised. Then he ran off with her children, bearing them back down the stairs.

The worst part, again, was at the doorway. He knew he couldn't entirely protect the children. He also knew the fastest way out would be to simply dive through the flames, but landing, with a little one in each arm, would be tricky. Instead, he stopped for a minute, put them down, convinced them to grip him around the middle, and wrapped his duster around them, holding them steady from outside it. He dashed through the flames and ran to where the neighbors waited, releasing the two kids into the care of someone they recognized through their tears.

He went back for the mother next. He found her in tears, right where he'd left her. When he told her that her children were safe, she smiled, but the tears continued running down her cheeks. He lifted her to his shoulder in the aptly named fireman's carry and hurried her outside. On the ground, she kissed Angel on the cheek and then threw her arms around her children.

He went back in. At the next apartment, when he kicked in the door he was met by a man with a gun. It looked like a semiautomatic pistol, and he held it at arm's length, in a hand that shook like a dog coming out of a swimming pool. "You keep outta here!" the guy cried when he saw Angel come through the doorway. He looked to be in his mid-thirties, spiky-haired and pale, his eyes wide and liquid with fear.

"I'm here to help you," Angel said reassuringly, holding up his hands to show that he was. "Is there anyone else in here? Any kids?"

"Just me, man," the guy answered angrily. "And you ain't touchin' my stuff."

"You have to get out of here," Angel insisted. "This whole place is going to come down."

"What's it to you?" he asked. He still held the gun out, and the shaking had subsided a little as he became more argumentative and less afraid.

Angel gave a shrug. "Nothing, I guess. You want to die in here, be my guest. I just wanted to help out if I could."

He started for the door when he heard a child's cry coming from behind a closed door. "What's that?" he demanded. "You have a kid in there?"

"Just let me be, man," the guy complained, shifting so he blocked the doorway. "I ain't done nothing to you."

"You're not letting a kid suffer because of your paranoid fantasies," Angel said. "Put the gun down and get out of my way."

The child wailed again, but the man didn't

budge. Angel didn't give him time to respond—
there were too many other apartments here, too
many other people feeling trapped by the flames in
the corridor and stairway. He charged in too fast
for the guy to track, swinging up with his left arm
as he did to deflect the gun and driving his right
fist into the man's solar plexus. A shot rang out but
flew harmlessly into the ceiling, and the guy dou-
bled over Angel's hand. Angel followed up with a
swift elbow into the chin, and the guy dropped
hard.

With him out of the way, Angel opened the door.
A young boy stood in a cluttered bedroom on the
other side, tears rolling down his face, looking up
at Angel with a mixture of terror and wonder. He
was probably ten, Angel guessed, and he clutched
a stuffed rabbit to his chest.

Behind him, one wall was completely hidden,
obscured by stacks of boxes containing high-end
electronics—TVs, stereos, DVD burners, and
more. *Probably knocked over a delivery truck,*
Angel thought, *and hasn't had a chance to fence
the stuff yet.*

"Everything'll be okay," Angel assured the boy.
"What's your rabbit's name?"

The boy swallowed and gulped. "He's Ch-
chester," he said.

"Well, hang on to Chester and hang on to me,"
Angel said. He scooped the boy into his arms and

carried him out of the bedroom, stepping over the unconscious man on the other side. "He's all right," Angel promised. "I'll come back and get him once you're safe. You and Chester. First things first."

"But . . . ," the boy said, his lip quivering. He trembled in Angel's arms. "But . . ."

"That your dad?"

The boy nodded. Angel tried to cover his sigh. Obviously the kid wasn't going to be happy unless they all went together. Glancing at the open door, Angel realized he was probably right—smoke billowed in from the corridor, and flames had started to climb the inside of the doorjamb. The apartment would be fully engulfed within minutes.

He bent down and lifted the unconscious man. The guy was skinny, but he was dead weight and he flopped around until Angel got him laid over his shoulder. Then, with the kid against his chest and his dad over him, Angel rushed out the door. A hot, fierce wind generated by the fire itself blew through the hall, searing Angel, sucking the moisture out of him. But he turned against it and carried his burdens to the stairs, then down and outside. Once again, the neighbors reacted with joy when they saw survivors appear, and a couple came to tend to the father, who was just starting to come around.

Angel left them both in the care of their neighbors and returned to the inferno.

In all, he went back into the building eleven times, bringing out one or two people on every trip. After the fourth time, the neighbors began to applaud him each time he returned, and the lady with the hose started watering him down every time she saw him. Finally, they assured him that everyone was out and accounted for. Sirens grew closer—he thought it was too late to save the block, but still, the fire needed to be contained before it spread to other buildings. Angel was tired, his hair singed, flesh and clothing scorched. But he had accomplished something.

Even though, he knew, it had been one more thing keeping him away from the Fletcher house.

He left the crowd behind and went back around the building, heading for the freeway and the car he had left there.

But before he reached it, five men emerged from the shadows, heavily armed and bearing wooden stakes.

"No one could've done all that," one of them said. "At least, no one human."

CHAPTER THIRTEEN

More of Lindley's fanatics, Angel thought. *Just what I need right now.* He shook his head slowly. "You really don't want to mess with me," he warned them.

"We're gonna mess you up," one of them, a big man with a flat silver crewcut, said.

"Duane's right," a smaller one added. "Just tell us, you a vamp or some other kinda demon?"

Angel let the change come over him—forehead rippling, fangs and claws extending. "Answer your question?"

"I told you, Billy," another one said. This one had a commanding kind of attitude. Angel guessed he was one of those people who said "I told you so" on a fairly regular basis. "Bloodsucker."

They were an odd group. Three of them wearing jeans and cowboy boots; the fourth, a burly, hairy guy, was in a lumberjack shirt; the fifth, a little man with neat creases in his clothes and a short, neat haircut. Since they were down the slope, facing him, and the fire was behind his back, they were illuminated by the shifting glow of the flames. The big lumberjack and the little guy stood off by themselves a little, away from the cowboys. Angel made eye contact with the smaller one.

"I'm betting you don't really know these others," he said, with a tilt of his head toward the cowboy-booted group.

"Not really," the guy admitted. "But we don't need to. We know what you are—that's what's important."

"You obviously don't know as much as you think you do," Angel said. "Do you know I just pulled a dozen or so people out of that burning building?"

"We know," the lumberjack said. His voice sounded educated, even cultured, in spite of his wild-man look. "We don't really understand that. Joe Ed there thinks you just like your dinner raw."

"Joe Ed there may be a moron," Angel suggested. "Did that cross your mind?"

"I have to say, it did," the lumberjack replied. "But that's really not the issue here."

"You think what?" the one Angel guessed was Joe Ed said with a snarl. He was the guy who seemed to be the leader of the cowboys.

The lumberjack shrugged. "I don't know you,"

179

he said. "Just know that you started the fire here, and there didn't seem to be any vampires in the building until this one happened along."

"Yeah," Joe Ed said. "And now you're standin' there talkin' to it instead of runnin' a stake through its heart like you ought to."

Angel sighed. He had hoped there was a way to get out of having to fight these guys. He was already bushed from the night and the fire, and still had a long way to go before he could get any rest. But Joe Ed wasn't going to make it easy on him, it seemed. He started to run through the fight in his head. Take down Joe Ed first, he thought, and his pals might fold. The other two guys, the ones who weren't with them, would probably run away at the first sign of real danger—though, he had to admit, they had held their ground when he'd gone all fangy on them.

But he was in for a surprise. He turned to rush Joe Ed, and the lumberjack, moving much faster than he'd expected just based on the guy's size and build, charged him with a stake in each fist. Angel switched tacks midstream and went into a defensive stance, legs wide, hands ready to meet the onslaught.

Even then, things didn't go as he expected. The lumberjack lunged at him, pistoning both stakes toward him. Angel kicked out and, because the guy was downslope from him, the kick caught him square in the middle of his plaid shirt. The man gave a grunt and tumbled backward. Before Angel's foot was back on the ground, though, two of the cowboys, the ones called Duane and Billy, were on him. Billy jumped up and got a grip on his ankle, jerking Angel's leg out from underneath him before he'd regained his balance from the kick, and Duane slammed a shoulder into his gut. The combination drove Angel down on his back with Duane on top of him.

Billy clawed his way up Angel's leg, jabbing at him with a sharp stake of his own. He was far from any fatal area, but the wounds hurt nonetheless. Angel tried to kick Billy away, but he couldn't see what he was doing because Duane blocked his view. The big man had a stake in his meaty fist, and he held it high, intending to bring it down fast and hard.

Angel bucked, sending Duane flying, then lashed out with his other leg and kicked Billy away. He scrambled to his feet before the others could attack, but not before Joe Ed had aimed a hunting rifle at him. Angel heard someone else coming up behind him, but figured he had a few moments to deal with that threat, and started to tell Joe Ed that his weapon was useless. Joe Ed fired before Angel could get a word out, and the first shot smashed into his shoulder. Angel groaned and his knees buckled, and Joe Ed's next shot flew above him, although if Angel hadn't fallen, it would have hit him in the face.

From behind, Angel heard a scream.

"Caleb!" the little guy cried out, running up behind Angel. Angel looked back as he struggled for his footing again on the grassy, scrubby hillside. The lumberjack, Caleb, apparently was on his back, blood gurgling from his throat, arms and legs quivering helplessly. "You shot Caleb!" the little guy screamed. He threw himself down on the big guy's body, hugging it and weeping.

The shot would be fatal. Angel couldn't do anything to help the big man. If there had been an ambulance close by, they possibly could have rushed him to a hospital in time, but the chances of that happening, tonight of all nights, were slim to none. And nothing short of a full-fledged emergency room or trauma center would help him.

He looked back at Joe Ed, who looked stricken and angry at the same time, as if he felt terrible about what had happened but blamed someone else.

Guess who? Angel thought.

"He turned to mist or somethin' and let it go right through him!" Joe Ed shouted. "My aim was as true as could be!"

"Your aim was off, and you know it," Angel said. He didn't disguise the menace in his voice now. "You killed a perfectly innocent man and you can't even admit you did it."

"It was you!" Joe Ed shot back. He raised the gun again.

"I've had just about enough of you," Angel warned. He threw himself down the slope at Joe Ed before the man could fire again. He landed hard, knocking both of them to the ground, and he batted the rifle away from Joe Ed's hands. Kneeling on Joe Ed's sternum, knees crushing his ribs, he let his fists fly, one hard punch after another after another. Joe Ed's face purpled, his cheek split open, blood spraying the leaves and brush underneath them.

After a minute of that, Angel realized he'd kill the guy if he wasn't careful. He climbed off Joe Ed, who curled into a ball, whimpering and pawing at his face. Joe Ed's pals stood back, hands at their sides, looking in horror at their friend.

Caleb had gone completely still, and his friend sobbed over the body.

"You'd better get an ambulance for him," Angel said, pointing at Joe Ed with one boot. "And tell the cops that he killed this other guy, Caleb. If I hear that you didn't, I'll tell them myself. Then I'll come after you." He looked again at Joe Ed's face, pulpy and ruined. "I didn't mean . . ."

He left the thought unfinished. He hadn't intended to do that much damage to the guy, he knew. But he'd done it, anyway. He'd let the frustrations of the night carry him away. He felt sick about it, but it was too late to do anything now except continue on, try his best to help as many people as he could. Joe Ed had killed a fellow human being—accidentally, perhaps, but as a result of his own misguided actions. He bore some of the responsibility, as did Angel, as did Mac Lindley. Angel would pay for it for an eternity, adding it to the scores of victims he already carried in his heart. Joe Ed would never look in a mirror without forgetting his complicity.

As Angel got back in his car, he hoped the others would be able to bring Mac Lindley to heel. If he saw the radio host, he'd probably lose control again.

And it wouldn't be a pretty sight.

CHAPTER FOURTEEN

Wesley drove. Fred rode shotgun, while Cordelia, Connor, and Lorne crowded into the backseat. Wesley was surprised at how much the situation in the city had continued to deteriorate since he'd arrived back at the Hyperion after visiting Willoughby. There were overturned cars and trucks along the roadway, smoke pouring from buildings, helicopters patrolling the sky like vultures searching for carrion. Looking at the destruction, he asked, "How could Mac Lindley have had so much impact on Los Angeles? He's just one man with a radio show. Certainly he has listeners, but this is as if barbarian hordes had overrun the city's walls."

"Maybe that's what it is," Lorne said. "Maybe civilization really is just a veneer and when you strip it away, expose what's underneath, it doesn't take much to return people to a barbarous state."

"Do you really believe that, Lorne?" Fred asked.

"Look at where I'm from, honey," Lorne reminded her. "My experience with barbarism is personal and recent."

He was right, Wesley realized. In Pylea, decapitation, while not always fatal, was not an uncommon way to deal with those considered to have broken the law, and even if the authorities didn't do it, one was equally likely to lose one's head in an ax fight or something, right in the town square.

So it was true that Lorne's insight into civilization, and its limitations, probably carried more weight than the rest of theirs. Equally likely, Wes supposed, he was at least partially right in this case. People had come to Los Angeles to fight monsters—their emotions probably mixed between terror at what they might find and justifiable anger over the idea that their homes, lives, and loved ones might be threatened. That combination was a virulent one, allowing those people—stirred up by Mac Lindley's ravings—the freedom, or so they believed, to ignore both law and common decency in their desperate attempt to keep themselves "secure." He hoped that those running rampant in the city now would reach the same conclusion, but assumed that they would not until they'd had a chance for sober reflection.

When they passed through El Monte, northeast

of downtown, traffic on the freeway came to a sudden stop. Wesley noticed the sea of brake lights in time to pull off at the nearest exit, and as they left the freeway he could see a gasoline truck on its side up ahead, blocking all the lanes of eastbound traffic. He was about to point it out to the others in the car when it suddenly exploded, a fireball shooting at least a hundred feet into the air, pieces of bent and twisted metal raining down all over the neighborhood.

"Good thing you got off the freeway, Wes," Connor said. "That was pretty gnarly."

"Yes, I believe 'gnarly' sums it up quite nicely," Wesley agreed. "However, now we face the problem of slow traffic on surface streets, since our best route to Norco seems no longer to be an option."

"Stay on this street to the 605 south," Lorne advised. "Then you can catch the 70 east. Works just as well as the 10. And maybe it hasn't been blown up."

"How do you know the freeways so well?" Wesley asked him. "You haven't lived here that long, really, and you rarely drive."

Lorne chuckled. "No, but I love those online mapping sites. You can learn the greatest things."

"Yeah," Fred agreed happily. "Lorne turned me on to those. And also, on those medical sites? You can find out about all kinds of diseases like bacteria

187

that eat human flesh and . . . well, maybe that's not exactly good conversational material."

"Perhaps not," Wesley said, relieved that she hadn't gone into more detail. He steered the car around a huge black Hummer that sat in the middle of a lane with its emergency blinkers flashing. When he glanced inside it, there was no one in view.

"But maybe you could show me, you know, later on?" Connor asked Fred.

"Sure, Connor. I'd be happy to."

"Just don't share with me," Cordelia asked. "I hate to think of my skin going two days without the proper moisturizers—a skin-eating disease would just be too awful to even consider."

Wesley tuned out the discussion—which was beginning to border on the too-inane-to-listen-to level, anyway—because he thought something more urgent was developing up ahead. He slowed the car. Traffic on this street was surprisingly light—given the time of night, he supposed, not all that surprising after all, but judging by the number of vehicles that had been on the freeway, it didn't seem like anyone in Los Angeles was sleeping tonight, or staying home. Probably, he guessed, everyone was trying to get out of town before the whole city burned to the ground.

Ahead, he thought he'd seen a strange, multi-part shadow from the cross street. He braked to a near stop and shushed his passengers, then slowly rolled to the corner. Everyone was alert now, looking out the window to see what had intrigued Wesley.

As he cleared the corner he realized that he'd been right. The shadow he had seen was made by a group of ten men. They looked like soldiers—short haircuts, camouflage uniforms. Marines, perhaps, or National Guard troops, he wasn't sure. But they carried wooden stakes, not guns—except for one armed with a crossbow and wooden bolts, much as Wesley himself often used. They were here to hunt, not to keep order. Perhaps they thought they were doing both.

The pair of vampires they had cornered against a pawnshop's barred window didn't see it that way, obviously.

"What should we do?" Fred asked. "We should do something. That isn't fair."

"Fair?" Connor echoed. "Those are vamps they're about to dust. We fight them, too, remember?"

"But the people who wounded you were vampire hunters just like them," Cordelia pointed out. "Maybe they've got actual vampires this time, but that doesn't mean they should be able to just go berserk."

"Cordy, they're on our side," Connor insisted. "Sure, some of them get a little carried away. But they're fighting for a good cause. We should be helping them, not trying to find a way to stop them."

"I understand, Fred," Wesley offered. "I feel for the underdog. But in this case, I think Connor's right. Those two are vampires. If those men don't dust them, then they'll be killing again by tomorrow night. And if we'd happened across them, we'd stake them too."

Fred frowned. "I know," she said. "But I just think the way we do it is better. More even. We don't usually gang up on them."

"Maybe we should, lambchop," Lorne suggested. "Safer for us, more deadly for them."

Wesley kept his foot on the brake, watching as the uniformed soldiers closed in on the vampires and ran stakes through their hearts. When the vampires exploded into the familiar dust clouds, he pressed down on the accelerator, intending to continue on course to Mac Lindley's location. At the sound of the engine gunning, though, several of the uniformed men turned around to see who had been watching them.

Which was when Wes noticed that each of them had four orange-pupiled eyes, in two sets of two, one above the other, and prominent horned ridges over the top pairs. "Blast," Wesley said, stepping on the brake. "Perhaps we should have interfered after all."

"They were still vamps," Connor pointed out.

"That's true," Wesley said. "But if demonic sects are taking advantage of this chaos to settle old scores, then no one is safe—human or otherwise."

"Wes has a point," Lorne agreed. "They look like Dashtars. Very angry types."

"But we need to find Mac Lindley," Fred reminded them.

"We will," Wesley promised. "Right after we deal with this." He turned off the ignition and popped the trunk, in which, since the car was full, they'd stored their weapons. "Let's be quick, every-one."

He threw his door open, and the others followed suit. From the trunk he drew an adz. Lorne, the next one back, took out a crossbow. "They've got one," he pointed out. "Can't let them have all the advantage."

Connor took a dirk, its short blade sharpened on both edges—but then, he liked close-up fighting. Cordelia helped herself to a broadsword that Wes wasn't even sure she'd be able to lift, but she handled it with practiced ease. Fred chose a small hatchet.

Seeing the weapons emerge from the trunk, the four-eyed demons in military garb charged them, except for the crossbow-wielding one, who took careful aim and let a bolt fly straight at Lorne. Lorne ducked behind the car and loosed a bolt of his own at his attacker. Wes and the others, mean-while, assumed defensive postures and waited for the onslaught.

Cordelia was a pace ahead of the rest, so she engaged the first Dashtar to reach them. The sol-dier demons only carried stakes, which seemed to put them at a disadvantage, but when they got close enough, Wesley saw that their mouths were full of tiny, needle-sharp teeth and their hands ended in jagged, curling claws. Blocking a thrust stake with her sword's blade, Cordy sidestepped jabbing claws and, with a whoop, sliced through the demon's neck. His head spun several times before dropping to the street, and yellow blood, as thick as house paint, spurted from its severed neck.

Then they were all engaged. Two of the soldiers stabbed at Wesley. He blocked one with the adz, but the other slipped past and the stake tore his shirt, scratching his chest. He winced and brought the handle of the adz down sharply into the demon's arm. The crunch and snap of bone was satisfying, as was the look of pain in all four of the demon's orange eyes. It gnashed its spiky teeth at him, but he put an end to that by bringing the blade of the adz down in a sweeping arc that split its head down the middle. The second attacker tried to take advantage of Wesley's divided focus, but Wes blocked a lunge with the adz's handle and kicked the demon in the gut. The Dashtar folded, and Wes brought the blade back around, slicing the demon in two.

When he looked up, Wes saw that the others in his group were meeting with similar success. Connor, in spite of his recent injury, was agile and ruthless, and with only his dirk had dispatched three of the demons. He currently struggled against a fourth, both combatants locked in hand-to-hand battle. Cordelia had split another one, and Fred's little hatchet had cleaved the skull of a Dashtar foolish enough to get within range of it. Even Lorne's crossbow battle had gone well—his foe had collapsed against the pawnshop's front door with two bolts in him, crossbow on the ground at his feet. As the rest looked on, Connor vanquished the last Dashtar and rose from the street, disheveled and spattered with yellow blood, but grinning madly. "That was fun," he said with obvious good cheer.

"Yes, well, with any luck we won't have to have that much fun again tonight," Wesley replied.

"Umm, Wes?" Lorne said hesitantly.

"Yes, Lorne?"

"You might want to check your wheels." Lorne pointed to the rear of the car, where two of the Dashtar's crossbow bolts had penetrated the sheet metal. "Sorry, Charlie," Lorne added.

Wes tossed him a grim smile. "Don't worry," he said. "It's a rental." *Charged,* he thought but didn't say, *on Lilah's credit card.*

Oh, well. Her problem, not mine.

He got back behind the wheel. "Buckle up, guys."

"There are winners and there are losers in the Night Country, people, but the biggest losers of all are those who don't even try. You might set out to stake a bloodsucker and get bit yourself for your trouble. Sad, but at least you tried. You put something higher than the protection of your own skin, and that makes you a hero, in my book. You could also sit in the dark in your living room with a gun in your hands, jumping at the slightest sound and finally shooting the paper boy when he goes to drop the daily news on your front step. That, my friends, is no hero at all. That's no winner."

Mac wiped his neck with a grimy rag. He was sweating like a pig tonight, but he didn't know why. Coming down with something, he guessed. He wasn't hot—he felt cold, in fact, kept having attacks of the shivers. He had downed cup after cup of coffee, trying to get warm, but it hadn't worked. The coffee just made him feel jittery, shaky.

Getting sick, he decided. That's what it was. He had stayed on the air too long, he hadn't been sleeping well. Now he was worried about his listeners, his friends from the Night Country who had gone to L.A. on his say-so and were getting mowed down by cops and monsters. He should have slept during the day, but instead he had kept broadcasting, trying to coordinate the efforts of his listeners as if he were some kind of general. He had worn himself out, and now he was paying the price.

"I know a lot of you are out there. Don't just listen to old Mac, check the twenty-four-hour cable news stations, the online news outlets. They'll tell you some of the story. Mass public disturbances in Los Angeles, they'll say. National Guard called out. Mayor declares state of emergency, governor flying down from Sacramento, every cop on the payroll of every law enforcement agency in the Southland out on the streets. Gun battles on the streets of Los Angeles, friends. Buildings on fire from Pomona to Pasadena. That's you, ladies and gents. You, who were not content to stay at home and wait for the monsters to come to you. You, who were bold enough to take action. You, who took to the streets to defend America."

He stopped, took another sip from a cup of coffee that had grown almost ice cold, and wiped his forehead with the rag. Yeah, probably getting sick, but there was more to it than that. He felt . . . strange. That was the best way he could put it. His whole body tingled, as if from static electricity. He felt bloated. He felt like something was happening, something was imminent, but he didn't know what. He wished Marie had been there—she would have been able to tell what was going on. Or Kara, who would, no doubt, have had friends who had been through the same thing. Mac had experienced enough paranormal events to know when another one was upon him, and it was tonight, that was for sure.

He didn't know what form it would take. But he knew it was coming. *Something* was coming.

"Denizens of the Night Country, you are the heroes here. You are the ones who stood beside America, who stood up for America when her hour of need was the darkest. None of us know what the dawn will bring. But thanks to your efforts, chances are it will arrive with many fewer vampires on the earth, with many fewer demons to threaten our way of life.

"From Alabama to Algeria, it will come. From Azerbaijan to Algodones, it will come. From Ashland to Amsterdam, it will come. From Afghanistan to Argentina, it will come. From Arkansas to Antarctica, it will come. From Alaska to Andorra, it will come."

Mac shook his head. He looked at the coffee cup beside him, but it had been drained. He didn't remember drinking it. He didn't remember a lot of things about this evening. He noticed a notepad on his console, one he usually used to jot down notes about things callers said that he wanted to respond to. But it had nothing that made any sense written on it. Someone—he didn't think it was him, but then, he was alone in here, had been all night—had drawn a picture of a long, thick, snake-looking thing with tendrils hanging off it, like long hair or tentacles. He—or whoever—had pressed down so hard that the pen had torn through the top three sheets of paper. Next to this little masterpiece, someone—or he—had written today's date, about a dozen times, one on top of another.

It was all a little weird. He had not the first memory of any of that. He touched his ribs to see if maybe he was feeling a little tender there, maybe there had been another abduction incident. It had been years since the last one, and the cuts didn't feel raw at all.

He took the microphone in his hand and shook his head as if to clear away the cobwebs. "Did old Mac say it was too late, ladies and gents? I don't think I said that at all. I didn't mean to say that. I don't think I said that. It's late, yes. But if you can get to L.A. before the sun comes up, then get in your truck, get in your car, get on your hog, get in that SUV, get in that mini-van with individual climate control and kiddie seats and DVD players, and get down there as fast as you can. You might still see some action, you might still be able to stake a bloodsucker or two. It's worth a try, isn't it?

"And if you can't make it tonight, well . . . there's always tomorrow night, right? I mean, tomorrow

night might be harder, because the authorities—
and we know how they like to muck things up,
right, let's not upset the status quo—they might
just get in the way and foul everything up like they
tend to do. So tonight is best. But this is not a
struggle that will be won in a single night, I can
guarantee you that. Our friends in the Night
Country have been at this for days and days now,
nights and nights, it's just that it's tonight that it's all
come to a head, hit critical mass, if you will. If you
can't get to L.A. until tomorrow, that's fine. Next
day, that's fine. You're still needed. From Bermuda
to Brisbane, it will arrive. So don't just sit there listening to old Mac if there's a way you could be
helping out. Get in the car. From Bellingham to
Britain, it will arrive. Bring wooden stakes, bring
silver bullets, bring garlic, bring holy water. Whatever you can carry. From Birmingham to Bristol, it
will arrive."

Dan snapped off the radio. Caleb was in the Jeep's
backseat—well, Caleb's body, anyway. Dan hadn't
decided yet what to do with it, but he knew he was
sick of listening to Mac Lindley. Guy had gotten
his best friend killed, the best friend he'd ever had,
or ever would have. He was probably loony to
begin with, Dan should have recognized that. But
he'd been getting worse, hour by hour, and now he
was just completely buggy. Dan figured he'd stick

to music stations from now on, leave the talk radio to someone else.

Caleb didn't have any kids, which would have made it worse. But there was still Sheila, Caleb's wife. She doted on the big lunk. If he had to explain to her what had happened, well, there'd be tears, there'd be screaming, there might even be cops, an investigation.

Jail.

Dan couldn't handle jail. Just could not take it. All those criminals. Living in a tiny cell. Dangerous people who'd as soon kill him as look at him. Rules and regulations—when to eat, when to sleep. He would hate it. Worse. He'd go insane. He'd curl up into a little ball, like a pill bug, like a porcupine, and he'd never come out again.

He hadn't wanted to find any action. That had been Caleb's objective. Dan had been driving around, hoping that they'd be too late, hoping that every incident crazy old Mac Lindley tried to send them to would have wrapped up before they reached it. As soon as they'd reached that place in Echo Park, hooked up with Joe Ed and Duane and Billy, Dan had feared the worst. Those guys were just as nutty as Mac Lindley, that was the impression he got. They were gung-ho to kill monsters. They claimed they'd already done some, already staked some vamps, and were ready to do it again. They had this whole plan worked out, had gasoline in cans and a building where they said vampires nested. They'd torch the place. Either the vamps would burn up inside or they'd come out, and if they came out, they could be staked.

Dan had wanted to get back in the Jeep and drive away, but Caleb thought it sounded great. He harangued Dan into sticking around. "It'll be fun," he'd said. "We'll learn the ropes from these guys, then we'll go off on our own and do some more. It's what we came for, right?"

Dan hadn't been able to argue with that. It was, indeed, what they had come for.

So Joe Ed and his pals had spread gasoline all around the building and then they'd lit it up. Fire blossomed fast; the ground must have been dry, the building lacking even the most basic sprinkler systems. But when the people had poured from it, screaming and crying, Dan had been horrified. They were people, just people. They had kids, families, pets. They weren't vampires. And when the people started to call out from inside, when the terrified nightmare screams echoed from those who were trapped, Dan's blood ran cold. *We're murderers*, he thought. *We're as bad as the vampires—if they even exist.*

It wasn't until the one guy kept running in and coming out with more people—*saving* people—that they realized he was something other than human. No human could have survived as many trips in there as he had, sucking smoke, with no safety equipment or anything. And no one could have been strong enough to make trip after trip carrying full-grown adults in his arms like they were toys.

So there *were* vampires. And they had found one. And the one they found was a freaking hero.

Dan had wanted to let him go. Joe Ed wouldn't hear of it. He had argued that a vampire was a vampire, and inherently evil, and if this one was rescuing people, it was just because he was trying to throw them off his track. They had confronted him, and he had been forced to fight them, in his own defense. And Joe Ed had shot Caleb—the vamp hadn't touched him, it had been that nutcase Joe Ed.

But Sheila wouldn't care about all that. Even if she believed it. All she'd be concerned about was that Caleb and Dan had gone to L.A. together, and only one was coming back alive.

So he drove east, headed for Interstate 15, which would lead through Las Vegas and Salt Lake City and finally up to Missoula. Sometime between here and there he'd have to figure out what to do with Caleb's body, and then he'd have to come up with some story to tell Sheila. Hopefully a convincing one, because Sheila tended to be a suspicious sort at the best of times, and she asked a lot of questions. This time, she'd ask more than usual,

and she'd certainly bring the cops in, maybe even
the FBI. And they'd ask a lot too. Dan had been
audited by the IRS once, and that had been nerve-
wracking enough. Caleb had tried to calm him
down, had coached him—he'd been through it
dozens of times, with clients, he said. But having
questions thrown at him like that, especially by
someone in authority, threw Dan for a loop. He
didn't know if he could stand talking to Sheila, and
then everything that would come in the wake of
that conversation.

But he'd be covering a lot of desert, between
here and Missoula. *Anything can happen in the
desert,* he thought. *Anything.*

CHAPTER FIFTEEN

After everyone else had left the scene, Joe Ed stuck his hands out toward Duane and Billy. "Help me up," he insisted. He could barely see the other guys. One of his eyes didn't seem to be working at all, and the other was filmed over with red. He touched his right eye, and a hot lance of pain shot through his head. His eye was swollen and puffy, and his hand came away slick with blood.

"But Joe Ed," Billy complained, "you heard what that guy said. We got to get you an ambulance. And call the cops."

"Forget the cops!" Joe Ed managed. "That dude took his pal's body, so there's nothing to report. And no freakin' ambulance either. That guy was a blood-sucker, and we gotta kill him before he gets away."

"Joe Ed," Duane said, shaking his head. "He's already away."

"How far could he have gone?" Joe Ed countered. "Traffic ain't movin', is it?" In fact, he was only guessing that was still the case, because it had been earlier. He couldn't see the road at all from here, and there was a roaring noise in his head that drowned out any sound from the cars. He was worried that the vampire had messed him up bad, maybe permanently.

But it could have been worse, he knew. The vampire could have killed him. Joe Ed was still surprised he hadn't. Wasn't that what vampires did, after all? Killing humans was supposed to be their thing. But this one had, it seemed, carried people from a burning building, and then, having fought them in self-defense, left them all alive. *Except for the one I shot,* he added mentally.

Maybe this one just hadn't been hungry. Maybe he had some other scheme, something that regular humans couldn't begin to understand. Must have been something like that, Joe Ed thought, because the guy was a monster, and monsters killed humans.

Joe Ed knew that the chance that he would die in Los Angeles had gone up considerably since taking on this particular bloodsucker. He also understood that it would increase geometrically if they found him again. He didn't feel any braver than he had before, any more anxious to leave Lorna and her kids behind for good. Maybe if he'd bought some insurance or something he'd feel differently, but they had come here so quickly, so spur of the moment, that there hadn't been time for anything like that.

She hadn't wanted them to come at all. She had cried when he'd told her they were leaving. He had tried to lie to her, to tell her they were going duck hunting. But she hadn't bought that for a second. She had wheedled and cajoled, and he had told her where they were going and why it was important.

Her first reaction had been laughter. But the more they talked, the more Lorna understood that there was nothing funny about it. He wasn't joking. The threat was real, and so was the danger he would face. That was when the laughter turned to tears, and she began to plead with him not to go. She even called Chantal, told her what was going on.

Lorna had not been able to dissuade Joe Ed, and Chantal hadn't even tried to talk Billy out of going. Finally, Lorna had become angry, as if it were some kind of personal affront. Like Joe Ed was just going to Los Angeles to get away from her. He figured that was a defensive reaction—that she had to take that attitude because it was easier than feeling sorrow at his leaving. It was nothing, he expected, to the grief she'd feel if the vampire killed him after all.

For that matter, he wouldn't exactly be happy about that himself.

Joe Ed stumbled on the brush and Duane caught him, but the jostling sent fresh waves of agony rolling through him. Maybe the beast hadn't killed him, but he'd come close. "Joe Ed," Billy said again. "You need a doctor or something. You look like somethin' my dogs drug home after they'd gnawed on it for a while."

"You think I was beautiful before we came here?" Joe Ed snapped. "Come on, get me to the truck."

Angel was tired of distractions, tired of traffic and roads blocked off, tired of the threat that Mac Lindley's minions posed to innocent life, human and otherwise, in his city. He had left the burning building behind, and the would-be vampire slayers who had waylaid him outside it, and continued his trek to the Fletcher house. If Gunn's somewhat far-fetched tale had any truth to it, getting back to the Fletchers' in a hurry was even more urgent than he had thought at first. But the roads hadn't improved any during his brief diversion. If anything, they were worse. Back at his GTX, he found that the congestion hadn't eased a bit on the freeway. So he exited as quickly as he could, only to find that a water main, broken by accident or explosion, had flooded a major intersection, had caused traffic to jam up on the streets he had intended to take instead.

He pulled into an alley, blessedly empty, and shot through it. The street parallel to the one he had left behind wasn't as crowded, but it was narrow and dead-ended a couple of blocks down. He pounded on the steering wheel in frustration and punched buttons on his radio, looking for a traffic report. Listening to Mac Lindley was doing him no good—he already knew the guy was a lunatic who needed to be stopped.

Performing a tight U-turn, he headed the other direction—back into traffic. Finally, after crawling for ten minutes, it broke up and he was able to start moving at a good clip again.

He had covered maybe ten miles when he stopped suddenly. Four vehicles—two pickups, a full-size SUV, and a sedan—had parked in such a way that the street narrowed to a single lane. From the shelter of the vehicles, men and women with guns and, in a couple of cases, hunting bows, made each car that tried to pass stop so they could check it out. They didn't look official, Angel thought, and neither did their roadblock. But he was in the line of traffic now, just four cars back, so he stayed in it. They wouldn't know at a glance that he was a vampire.

It wasn't until he was braking at the roadblock, his window open like the other motorists, his "innocent" smile on his face, that he noticed the crosses they carried. "I heard L.A. was a crazy place," he said, "but the travel agent didn't say anything about this kinda stuff. Is it like this every week?"

The two hard-faced men inspecting the cars didn't crack a smile or respond. They shone flashlights into the car, which Angel knew would never pass as a rental. Behind them, the ones with guns and bows stayed back, keeping to angles where they could get clear shots at Angel if they needed to. The one nearest Angel held the flashlight beaming into Angel's eyes while he pressed a small crucifix against the back of Angel's hand.

Angel's flesh hissed and burned where the cross touched it.

The car ahead of him had already pulled away, so Angel yanked his arm back in through his window and stomped on the gas. The GTX lurched forward, but the people staffing the roadblock were already in motion too. Bullets spanged off the sides. He had the top up, but it offered little resistance, and he could hear the whistle of bullets rushing past him, shattering the rear window and going out the soft top. He leaned over the wheel, trying to present as small a target as possible. A bullet in the back of the head would be a definite inconvenience.

As he screeched around a corner and punched

the car down the next couple of blocks, he checked his rearview mirror and was surprised to see that there was no pursuit.

With a shrug, he continued toward the Fletcher house.

The LAPD had a kind of habit of getting involved in terrible events—often through no fault of its own, believed Ron Helvand, who considered himself a kind of amateur sociologist as a result of the many things he had encountered during his years on the job. Sure, the Rampart scandal had been entirely self-inflicted, and so too had been the city's response to the Rodney King incident. But the Watts riots, the O. J. Simpson case, more recently the Robert Blake case, the occasional discovery of bodies drained of their blood through small holes in the neck—these were outside factors that the force had to contend with, not things they had brought upon themselves.

He had a feeling that the Fletcher house incident would join that catalog of departmental legends—if he and Julia survived to tell anyone about it. They had entered a perfectly normal suburban house—normal, if a little small for this particular neighborhood—that just happened to be the scene of a mass murder. Okay, not unheard of in the annals of police work. But then the doors and windows had gone away, replaced with some kind of impenetrable membrane.

A bit stranger, but still not completely without precedent. In other cities, maybe it would be news, but not in this one.

And then things had gone really weird.

"Ron . . . ?" Julia clutched his forearm, startling him. He liked the sensation. Any physical contact initiated by Julia was one of life's little rewards, as far as he was concerned. In fact, he kept hoping that the situation would drive them together, as sometimes happened when two people lived through a dangerous time. So far, however, if anything, it had had the opposite effect. Julia was folding into herself, walking with her arms wrapped around her torso, gazing down, as if she could isolate herself from whatever was going on around them and will herself back outside.

So when she grabbed him, it was a surprise. He followed her gaze. They had been walking aimlessly around the house, for lack of anything better to do, hoping maybe to find an exit they had somehow missed before, although that hadn't been a spoken plan. They had passed through the doorway into what had once been the living room, where the body was that they believed was Herman Fletcher's, with Julia a couple of steps in the lead.

But now, the living room wasn't even remotely recognizable. The cheap carpeting was gone, and in its place was a smooth, wet-looking pink floor that reminded Ron of the tongue of Andy, the German shepherd he'd had as a kid. *Or maybe,* he thought, *like someone dumped the world's biggest bottle of Pepto-Bismol.* The walls were still wall-like, mostly, but the pink material that made up the floor had climbed about ten inches up them, and seemed to be ascending still higher as they stood there watching it.

"It's . . . changing," Julia said.

"Yeah," Ron agreed. It was almost belaboring the obvious to even mention it, but Ron was beyond worrying about such petty concerns. It *was* changing; right in front of their faces, the room was becoming something . . . other.

Cops were supposed to be observant. He was trying to be, but the stuff that was going on here was so far outside the realm of what he even considered possible that it was hard to know exactly what he should be observing. "This has been weird for a long time, Julia," he said. "But now . . . I don't know. Beyond weird."

She nodded her head. He liked that, liked to see her hair bob when she did, liked the way her profile looked when her brow was furrowed in concentration, her full lips clamped tightly together. "Past weird into downright terrifying," she agreed.

Terrifying wasn't something he wanted to admit to. He wanted to be the pillar of strength, the guy she could depend on in the toughest spot either of them had seen. But in fact, he couldn't bring himself to deny it. "Yeah," he admitted. Under his feet, the floor was beginning to lighten, to take on a pinkish cast. "Yeah, terrifying. Good word for it."

". . . reports keep flooding in from the Night Country's war on monsters, and while we have a few sad stories, there are also notable successes being described. From County Cork to Kentucky, it will emerge. Here's a shout-out to Joe Ed and the boys, your target's been sighted heading west on Beverly Boulevard, delaying maneuvers in effect, but you'd better get a move on. From Mount Kilimanjaro to Macon, it will emerge. . . ."

"Merv Willoughby told me that Mac Lindley had always been gullible," Wesley said, talking over the voice that droned from the radio. "He was the sort of person who always looked for a more complex answer, who would always assume a conspiracy in the absence of proof positive to the contrary. If a cashier counted his change wrong, he would put it down to a plot to defraud him rather than to simple human error. Of course, he saw government as one huge collusion of interests dedicated to making him as miserable as possible. Eventually, according to Willoughby, the machinations of humans could no longer explain everything that Lindley perceived as being wrong with the world. That's when he started to focus his attention on the occult, the paranormal, and visitors from other planets and other planes."

"So his interest in all this spook stuff just comes from deep-seated paranoia," Lorne interpreted, "instead of from any personal experience with it." He'd encountered similar attitudes many times, even from demons who distrusted demons of different types without having actually ever interacted with them. Running Caritas, his former demon sanctuary nightclub, had been nothing if not educational.

"Well, in the years since," Wes replied, "he claims to have had run-ins with various sorts of occult phenomena. Shapeshifters, apparitions, extraterrestrials—apparently he's absolutely convinced that he has a series of implants in his body, left there by alien visitors."

"Does Mr. Willoughby believe him?" Fred asked.

Traffic this far out of the city was light, and the miles raced by. Wes kept a close watch on the roadway ahead, and Lorne found himself checking out the rear window often, just in case. He figured maybe there were times when paranoia was perfectly justified, and this, by every conceivable measure, was one of those times.

"Mr. Willoughby seems to believe that Mac Lindley is delusional," Wesley said. "He thinks Lindley really does believe the things that he says have happened to him. But Willoughby is a practical man, and he doesn't think there's any truth to Lindley's more arcane beliefs. Apparently, however, Lindley clings to them rather tenaciously, even at a high personal cost. He's been fired from more than one radio job because he won't stop talking about such things, even when he's supposed to be hosting a sports chat program, or news or some other topic."

"A man whose personal convictions are more important than the almighty buck," Lorne observed. "You almost have to admire it."

"Almost," Connor said. "Except for the part where his convictions are crazy, and there's nothing wrong with earning a living."

"Connor," Cordelia put in. "I'm with you on the making a living part, but his convictions are actually more correct than not. Or do I need to remind you that your parents were both vampires, and you're riding in a car with a former higher being and a green demon from Pylea?"

"Okay, yeah, two points," Connor admitted. "But we don't know any Martians or Venusians or anything, right?"

"There's evidence of ancient water on Mars, though," Fred pointed out. "Where there's water, there might have been life—at least at one point."

"I don't think alien microbes would have implanted stuff in the guy," Connor said.

"That probably requires opposable thumbs," Wesley agreed, nodding. "At any rate, Merv Willoughby thinks that Lindley has gone off the deep end now that his radio career is over, and that this is his version of going out with a bang."

"A lot of bangs," Lorne said. "And some booms and other loud noises too. I haven't seen so many fireworks in L.A. since the Fourth of July."

"Only people don't get hurt by that kind," Cordelia noted. "Except, you know, for the occasional fireworks warehouse explosion, or the accidental blowing up on the ground ones."

"I guess we'll know very shortly what Lindley's mental state is like," Wes said. He inclined his head toward an upcoming freeway exit. "We're almost there."

Angel made a right turn off Beverly Boulevard, intending to cut up to Santa Monica Boulevard, which the radio reported was flowing as freely as any major artery tonight. But as soon as he turned, a little red sports car whipped around the corner right behind him, shot past, then braked suddenly, fishtailing all over the street. *Idiot!* Angel thought. He tried to swerve around it, but the other car came to a sudden halt directly in front of him. To avoid hitting it, Angel had to yank hard to the right and pull up onto the sidewalk. A fire hydrant and a row of newspaper stands blocked his way, but he managed to brake before hitting them. The street was typical L.A. commercial, probably with apartments above the storefronts, and a row of palms, trunks lean and straight, tops towering somewhere above the glow from the streetlights.

Two men climbed up out of the low-slung sports car and walked toward him. The driver wore a loud Hawaiian shirt, and jeans with the knees torn out; the other one a black nylon track suit and a porkpie hat. The driver shook his head slowly. "You okay, dude?" he asked.

"I'm fine," Angel said. "And I'm kind of in a hurry."

"We need to exchange, you know, insurance information and stuff," the driver said.

Angel had never worried about things like having a valid driver's license or insurance. He didn't know if the guy in the Hawaiian shirt was drunk or what, but clearly he had been driving badly and the entire incident was his fault. "We didn't actually hit each other," Angel pointed out. "And, like I said, I'm in a hurry."

But by now, the guy was standing next to his car, leaning on it, looking down its length at the fresh bullet scars. The passenger in the track suit poked a long index finger through one of the holes in the roof. "Dude," he said. "Guess you're glad it don't rain much around here."

"Look, I know we didn't, like, make contact," the

driver said, leaning in toward Angel. He was blocking the door now, Angel noted, and the guy in the track suit blocked the other door. If Angel wanted to get out of the car, he'd have to go through one of them. "But you know, with a sports car and all, the cops and the insurance companies are really picky. We've had an incident, even if it's not really an accident."

Angel had run out of patience. "It's not an incident or an accident yet," he said. "It's you being in my way. But you're going to get out of my way or we'll have an incident and an accident, and you won't be happy about either."

The driver whistled and made eye contact with his friend. "Guy's got a lot of anger issues," he said.

"I know a dude," his friend offered. "Gives these seminars, over in Westwood. Anger management, calmness training. Kind of a mellow coach, what I call him. I could give you his number, if you want."

Angel put the GTX in reverse. Obviously these guys weren't going to get out of his way, and he couldn't go forward. He'd just have to back off the sidewalk and go around the sports car blocking both lanes.

But before he was able to do that, more people broke from the shadows and took up positions behind the car. He couldn't back up without running over them. *Which is starting to look pretty appealing,* he thought furiously.

Angel couldn't tell through the rearview mirror how many were behind him, and he didn't want to turn around, didn't want to take his attention away from the people who were close enough to attack him through his open windows.

The guy in the track suit had the safer position. Angel would have had to go all the way across his front seat to go out the passenger door. Which meant it was Hawaiian shirt who'd be going down.

First, at least.

Angel snatched at the door handle and shoved the door open in the same motion. The door caught Hawaiian shirt by surprise, slamming into his hip. Before he could even react, Angel was out of the car, driving his fist into the guy's jaw. It connected with a solid crack, and the man's head snapped sideways, his eyes rolling up in their sockets.

The man crumpled to the sidewalk. Angel turned toward his friend, who was the nearest other threat. He still stood on the other side of the GTX, but now there was a crucifix in his left hand and a stake in his right.

The people approaching from behind the car had pretty much the same accessories, with minor variations.

Just perfect, Angel thought, rage building in him again. *Still more of Mac's minions, out to screw up my night. I'll never get to the Fletcher place if I have to keep fighting these dopes.*

He was making his battle plan when a truck swung around the corner and came to a stop behind the GTX, its headlights beaming right at him. Three men emerged from the truck and walked forward, into the light. Angel recognized them.

Especially the one who looked like he'd been making out with a meat grinder.

"I didn't think I'd see you again, Joe Ed," Angel said. "I thought maybe you'd had some sense beaten into you."

Joe Ed tried to smile. It looked like it hurt. "You thought wrong, vampire. Way wrong."

CHAPTER SIXTEEN

Just looking at Joe Ed made Angel wince inside. The man's bruises were pulpy and red. Angel knew he had punished the man, maybe excessively, taking out the frustration of a long and terrible night on him. *But then again,* he thought, *he did shoot someone. He really belongs in jail, not out on the streets.*

Joe Ed seemed to have no such misgivings about the way he'd treated Angel—except, apparently, some leftover unhappiness that he hadn't been able to put a stake in Angel's heart.

Angel wasn't sure how Joe Ed had been able to find him. Last time he'd seen the guy, he was on his back, not looking like he was going to be up and around anytime soon. But here he was, a little wobbly on his feet, the puffy flesh around one eye swelling it shut, but scowling and with a fistful of wood.

From the looks of it, it was an organized effort. Hawaiian shirt and track suit had kept him pinned here long enough for Joe Ed and his friends to catch up. The other people who had surrounded the car were obviously in on it too. They shouted words of encouragement to one another, and threats toward Angel. He suspected the guiding hand of Mac Lindley behind this. He had probably kept everyone apprised of Angel's location since it seemed unlikely that all these very different people—some local, like the ones in the red sports car, and others, definite out-of-towners— had a way to communicate directly.

There were at least a dozen armed men surrounding him, though, and they knew he was a vampire. They carried crosses and stakes. He didn't have surprise on his side, or the supernatural terror he could sometimes use to advantage against opponents who weren't prepared for his transformation. It was the very fact that he was a vampire that had brought these people together against him.

And he was near exhaustion, still hurting from the bullet he'd taken earlier, anxious to get out to the Fletcher home.

What he needed was a plan, and he was fresh out of those.

Yeah, he thought, *but then I've never been that good at them, anyway.*

Instead of putting a lot of thought into it, he figured he'd take out Joe Ed first. If this all revolved around him, then maybe by putting him down—again—he would put an end to it. It wasn't really a plan so much as a notion, but it would have to do.

And if he was wrong, then he'd have a fight on his hands.

He hurled himself at Joe Ed, at a speed he knew most humans couldn't even follow. Joe Ed was still raising his hands defensively when Angel leaped into the air. Airborne, he landed two fast kicks, one to Joe Ed's chest and one to his ribs. Joe Ed staggered back against the hood of his truck. The stake he had gripped flew from his hand into the street.

Angel landed lightly, coiled and ready for more. But more wasn't coming from Joe Ed. He was bent over double now, clutching at the truck for support, his other hand held across his middle. If he hadn't needed hospitalizing before, Angel was convinced he did now.

He just hoped the stubborn man realized it.

After Joe Ed, the guy in the track suit was the next most dangerous threat, Angel determined. He was moving in fast and without apparent fear, a long, sharp stake in each hand. He held them like an experienced knife fighter—low and thrusting up, rather than overhand attacks that could be more easily blocked.

Angel waited for him to get close and then spun

out of his reach, letting his foe pass him. He ended his spin behind the guy, whose head swiveled as he tried to figure out where Angel had gone. Angel let him know with a quick one-two punch to the kidneys, and then as the guy started to turn, with a right to the jaw that flattened him.

It's easier to fight demons, Angel realized. He had to pull his punches enough so that he didn't kill these people. They couldn't take the kind of punishment that demons and vamps could, and Angel's intent in those battles was death. Now, he just wanted to put enough of his opponents out of commission that the rest would decide to let him go.

During the time it took him to dispatch Joe Ed and the guy in the track suit, the others had formulated something that looked suspiciously like a plan. Six of them closed at once, stakes out before them like thorns on a cactus. There was no place Angel could turn where there wasn't sharpened wood seeking him out. Except up—he could go over their heads. But that would only delay the inevitable, not forestall it.

Instead, he reached out and caught two shirtfronts at random. Squatting suddenly and bunching his arms, he drew those two people in toward him, breaking the symmetrical formation of the circle. With those two off-balance, he snapped them together so that their heads collided with a *thud.* Blood sprayed from one's nose and mouth, and the other went momentarily limp.

Angel held them in place while the rest of the former circle crowded around, all somewhat off-balance now because they were trying to stab down at Angel, who was protected by the bodies of two of their own. He felt the searing pain of stakes biting into his flesh, but none could reach the critical spot. At the optimal moment, Angel rose and hurled the two head-ramming victims into the air. The others in the circle fell back, a couple even dropping to the sidewalk. With the circle broken, Angel launched into a spin, kicking out at those who were still within range. One, two, three boots landed, three went down.

The others kept their distance, having seen how difficult it was to beat Angel in close quarters. Their stakes wouldn't do them any good as distance weapons; there were no crossbows in this crowd, or hunting bows with wooden arrows. But Duane, solid and silver-haired, had taken a shotgun from the truck and trained it on Angel's middle.

A hush fell over the remaining few. A stew of sweat, fear, blood, and broken flesh hung in the air. The sound of a shell being jacked into the shotgun's chamber was loud.

"You know if you fire that you'll injure or kill some of these people," Angel warned Duane. "Just like Joe Ed did." Even though the people had dropped back, putting distance between themselves and Angel, they still basically formed a circle around him. At this range, Angel's body would take a good deal of the shot from Duane's gun, but not all of it. Those behind Angel would feel it too.

"That's no concern of mine," Duane answered. "I don't know them. Just know what you did to Joe Ed, and what you are. We don't stop you now, who will?"

"And you think that'll stop me?" Angel touched his shoulder, where he knew Duane had seen him take a bullet earlier in the evening.

"Figure I knock out enough of your spine, it'll slow you down some."

He had a point.

Which made two reasons why Angel couldn't let him pull that trigger. He was trying, in spite of current circumstance, to keep these people alive. And he didn't particularly want to test Duane's hypothesis.

Bleeding from at least a dozen wounds, battered and bruised, he hoped he still had the necessary speed. Just in case, instead of going straight toward Duane—and straight into the blast, if he was able to squeeze the trigger in time—Angel went backward, up onto the trunk of his handy GTX. From there, he launched himself, somersaulting in midair. Duane raised the barrel of his gun to track him, but before he was able to get a shot off, Angel's booted feet were landing in his face.

Both of them went down in a tangle, and the shotgun clattered across the pavement. Angel lashed out with his fists, connecting with Duane's face and midsection. Duane responded with grunts and groans, and his own hands flailed ineffectually at Angel. Finally, his arms dropped to the ground.

Angel looked up into the barrel of the same shotgun. Joe Ed, sitting on the street with his back against his truck's front bumper, held it in shaking hands. Billy stood beside him, cutting the river of light from one of the headlamps.

"That's enough, vampire," Joe Ed said, his voice choked and gravelly. "Back off of him."

"Haven't you learned yet?" Angel asked. At a crouch, he slowly moved away from Duane's still form. "You're a hard man to teach a lesson to."

"Heard that in high school too," Joe Ed admitted.

"You fire that gun, you'll regret it," Angel cautioned. But then, if Joe Ed took the suffering of others seriously, he wouldn't be here after what he'd already done tonight. "Anyway, you know I can take it away from you before you can shoot me."

"I reckon so," Joe Ed said. He shifted the barrel away from Angel, pointing it instead up at Billy, standing right beside him. "But can you get to me before the shot kills him?"

"Joe Ed," Billy said, voice quaking. "What are you doin'?"

"Don't worry about it, Billy. What do you think, vampire? Can you make it in time? I don't think so."

Angel measured the distance he'd have to cross. Ten feet. Billy was only two from the end of the gun. If Joe Ed closed his finger on the trigger, even if Angel made it there before the shot burst from the muzzle, Billy would still take most of the load.

"Tell you what, vampire," Joe Ed continued when Angel didn't answer him. "You just stand there and let one of us run a stake through your heart. You do that, I won't shoot Billy. You really were concerned about saving folks instead of killing 'em, you'd go along with me."

My life for one other? Angel thought. *It's not worth it. I can save a dozen lives in one night, sometimes more. What has Billy accomplished tonight?*

At the same time, he knew he couldn't just stand there and let Billy die. If it had been anyone but Joe Ed, Angel would have thought he was bluffing. Joe Ed, though, had already proven his willingness to kill in order to claim victory over a vampire. Now—seriously injured, probably bleeding internally—this was the only way he could win.

He won't win, Angel decided. *He can't.*

Drawing on what he figured were his last reserves of strength and speed, he moved.

As if in slow motion, Angel saw Joe Ed's knuckle whiten as he applied pressure to the shotgun's trigger. He saw Billy's face collapse with horror, eyes going wide, jaw slackening. He saw himself, flying across the open space.

But not toward Joe Ed.

Instead, Angel hurtled himself from his crouching position, covering the space low to the ground. He hurtled into Billy's legs, heard bone snap in one of them, and drove Billy backward. Billy's skull slammed into the street, hard, and he let out a cry that was drowned out by the roar of the shotgun, its barrel pointed toward empty sky.

Angel came up off Billy and snatched the gun away from Joe Ed, holding it by its hot barrel. "That's enough," Angel said. "Enough of you and guns, enough of you and me. Go home, go check into a hospital, I don't care. Just don't let me see your face again."

The other would-be vampire hunters were already scattering, heading for cars or back into the shadows from where they had come. Joe Ed just sat there against the truck with a crestfallen look.

Slowly, Billy dragged himself up off the pavement. "I don't know what your story is," he said through pulped and swollen lips. "But I gotta think I was wrong about you. You may be a stinkin' vampire, but you got something else in you, I guess . . .

some kind of decency. We won't trouble you no more, you got my word on that."

Angel knew that he should acknowledge Billy's change of heart in some way. He hoped the guy could keep Joe Ed in line. Mostly, he wanted to punch Joe Ed in the mouth again, but he had already done enough of that. And he wasn't exactly a talkative guy at the best of times. Instead of answering, he simply turned, showing Joe Ed his back, and got back into his waiting car.

"Ia shob noggoth kla from Pasadena kalistu krianne. Tekeli-li from R'lyeh shog-thototh China Cleveland Casper azathoth ia ia. From Mulholland Laurel Coldwater astaroth kinnific ia sother sothem tetragrammatron an sint unquam daemones Beverly Trousdale Bel Air ia cantotum."

Mac reached for the rag, hoping to wipe the sweat from his brow before it dripped into his eyes, stinging and blinding him. But the rag was sopping wet now, sitting on the console in a puddle of its own making. Instead, he got up from his chair and ran some water from the tap into a pail he had—glasses were no longer big enough—and then carried the pail back to the console. He had consumed all the coffee in the place, and a twelve-pack of soda, but he was still thirsty, so thirsty. He drained half the pail, set it down next to the chair, and turned to the mic.

"Ia nisteroth klattur from Fox Hills from Manhattan Beach from Torrance ia efficiut daemones ut quae non sut. Sic tamen quasi sint from Carson from Culver from Mar Vista conspicienda bominibus exhibeant."

Mac reached for the pail again, downed the rest of the water. It seemed piped directly to his sweat glands. His shirt was soaked. He didn't understand a word of what he had just said, but that was nothing new—that had been the case for at least an hour now. At first he had worried about that, but not anymore. Something was happening to him, no question about that, and probably not anything good. But it was, quite obviously, beyond his control. Things had been set into motion, and he was an unwitting participant, with no more say over it than a screwdriver or a hammer had over the shape of a house they were being used to build.

He was a tool, but he was a thirsty tool.

He turned back to the sink, but he had left it running and only a trickle ran from the faucet now. He wasn't hooked up to the city water supply, had only what his trailer's storage tanks could hold, and that was all down in the waste tank now. He stuck his head under the tap, lapping up what he could, but within seconds even that faint stream ran dry.

Dead air. Too much dead air was the ultimate sin in the radio world. Mac hurried back to the mic, snatched the wet rag off the console, wrung some of the precious water into his mouth.

"Ia ia ross tutheroth nistria keletim-ti from South Central from Hancock Park from Westwood ia tulusto. Ia athanatos agyros ischryos nul testamon."

Doorways. When he closed his eyes he saw doorways, dark on one side—on this side, the side he was on in the bizarre waking vision—and bright on the other, sun-bright, light streaming in like water through the opened porthole of a submarine.

He didn't know what it all meant, didn't know what any of it meant. All he knew was that he was losing himself. He had a name, but he couldn't remember it. He was so thirsty. . . .

"Fenneroth ia constantinus cria from Sherman Oaks from Encino from Hawthorne ia azatoth mordido sleyn . . ."

"Can you turn that up, peanut?" Lorne asked from the backseat. Fred leaned forward and twisted the dial.

"What does it all mean?" Connor asked.

Fred glanced back and saw Lorne, his expression suddenly serious. "That's a deep question, sports fan. But I see where you're coming from. You want my take on it, I'd say it's about how you live your life, not what comes after it. Did you make those around you glad you were there? Did you go out of your way to help out a friend, or better yet, a stranger? Did you leave the world happier than when you came into it? Did you love others and let them love you? Did you try not to hurt? If you can answer yes to those questions, then I think you've got a good handle on what it's about. That's what it all means. At least, that's the gospel according to Lorne."

"Yeah, cool," Connor said. "But I meant, what the guy on the radio is saying."

"Oh, that? It's gibberish."

"It's not gibberish," Wesley corrected.

"Some of it's Latin," Fred pointed out.

"I didn't notice when it happened, precisely," Wesley went on. "But apparently at some point he went into his incantation full-time."

"It sounds like gibberish to me," Cordelia announced. *She's been oddly quiet tonight,* Fred thought. *Probably worried about Connor.* She couldn't begin to understand the relationship between those two since Cordelia had returned and regained at least some of her memory. But still, most of the time she acted more or less like the old Cordy, except for the huge crushing-on-Angel part. Tonight, though, something seemed to be throwing her off her stride. Maybe it was just Connor's injury, or maybe it was the whole thing with Mac Lindley. Fred couldn't really hazard a guess, but she worried about her friend just the same. "Or nonsense or whatever."

"Believe me," Wesley said. "It's not. To our ears, perhaps. But to the ears that matter, I'm sure there's a very precise meaning to every word. And it's likely still coming out of tens of thousands of radios, all over the city—even farther, considering the reach of Lindley's signal. It's perhaps the most widespread incantation in history."

"Which makes it especially bad news," Lorne added.

"Indeed. I believe we're there—we'd better hope we've come in time," Wesley said. He turned the car onto a dirt lane. At the end of it, in a wide circle of earth, stood a battered aluminum-sided mobile home. Atop and surrounding the mobile home were a variety of antennas, both towers and saucers.

"This has to be the place," Fred agreed. As Wesley braked the car in the dirt, a sudden chill fell over her and she wished Charles were there with them—not out of any leftover romantic connection, but because he was strong and brave and probably the best fighter of them all, except for Angel. She didn't know what they would find inside that motor home. But she was certain that it would be bad.

CHAPTER SEVENTEEN

As Angel steered his car up the hill through Beverly Glen, he saw stranger and stranger sights. Hallucinations, he had decided, created by whatever force was behind all the recent events. A hillside mansion exploded into purple flames before him. A huge reptilian beast, like a Tyrannosaurus rex brought back to life, stalked a side street, roaring and knocking over trees with slashes of his mighty tail. A host of winged vampires shot through the sky, their eyes glowing like tiny spots of fire. The road ahead buckled and swayed as if blown by a high wind. Whatever force was trying to delay his return to the Fletcher house, it was throwing everything it had at him now. But Angel would brook no more delays, would let nothing divert him from what needed to be done. He was close, he remembered the scenery from his last trip up the hill to Oak Tree Lane. He passed the alley where he had fought the two vampires who weren't vampires—the first diversion. The one that had bought somebody time to kill the Fletcher family. Tonight, the alley was littered with bleeding bodies. Angel looked at them, shrugged, kept going. *Another illusion.*

A few minutes later he turned up the drive. There were half a dozen police cars in front of the house, and cops sitting around staring at the place as if it might reveal its secrets to them if they only knew how to ask. Arc lights on stanchions, powered by a noisy generator, flooded the house's facade with light. The cops stared at Angel as he drove in and parked in the same place he had before. Ignoring their shouts, he took a sword from the trunk and headed for the house. Only before, there had been a front door. Now it was only a smooth surface, all painted the same. No door, no windows.

The house had sealed itself off.

Worse, horrible noises came from inside—creaking, groaning sounds, screams that sounded like metal grating against metal, and a mournful wail like a wind blowing across the emptiest, saddest landscape on Earth.

He reached into his duster's inside pocket, but his phone wasn't there. He then recalled dropping it on the passenger seat after talking to Fred. It seemed like a year ago. He returned to the car.

There was only one person he knew he could call on right now to help him. He hated to do it, hated to admit that he needed him. But he dialed Wesley's number. Cops headed toward him, a couple drawing weapons, as he listened to it ring.

"Angel," Wesley said when he answered. "We've just arrived at Mac Lindley's broadcasting . . . umm, trailer. We're about to go in, you just caught us."

"I need some help, Wes," Angel said urgently. "I'm at the Fletcher house, but . . . the door's gone. Windows, too. I can't see any way in." He had encountered this sort of situation before, and knew there was a spell that would get him inside. He couldn't for the life of him remember what it was. He also knew that spells reacted with one another in different ways—the spell that opened one door might not open another, if it had been sealed in a dissimilar fashion. But he had to try. He was even more convinced now that whatever was going on tonight was centered inside that house.

"Right," Wesley said. He sounded like he understood the situation instantly, which was one of Wes's strong points. Angel wasn't always thrilled with his ideas, but Wesley Wyndam-Pryce was one of the smartest people he had ever known. And in just shy of two and a half centuries, he had known a lot of people. "Try this."

Wesley recited a spell, obviously just off the top

of his head, which both astounded and relieved Angel. He had been afraid that Wes would have to look something up. This was better, though, faster. He echoed Wes's strange words, not understanding the meaning, but knowing that didn't matter. When it came to magick, it was the speaking of them that was crucial, not the comprehension.

As soon as he had finished the first phrase, the house fell silent. Angel was disturbed by that, because it seemed to indicate that the house, or whatever was inside it, knew he was there. But he was also heartened because it meant the spell was already having some effect. Wesley kept going and Angel kept repeating the words, shouting them toward where the door had once been. It was only a few phrases long, he was gratified to discover. He thought it was ancient Sumerian, but he wasn't positive.

It didn't matter. What mattered was that, as soon as he was finished, the texture of the house's outside surface changed in the places where the door and windows had been. Those spots became semi-translucent, as if clogged with thick jelly of some kind, no longer as solid looking as they had been. Angel described it to Wesley.

"Go in quickly, before it changes back," Wes urged him. "And good luck!"

Angel disconnected and stuffed the phone into his pocket. The cops had surrounded him. "This is a crime scene," one of them said. "I don't know what you think you're doing here, but if you know anything about this house, you're going to have to talk to us."

"No time," Angel replied simply. Grabbing the sword again, he ran from the car, dodging shouting cops like a running back heading for the goal line, and dove through the gelatinous mass before him. It didn't feel like jelly, but like some kind of hot electrical charge. It didn't block his way, however, and when he regained his footing, he was inside.

Inside what, he couldn't say. It had looked, on the outside, more or less like the Fletcher house, which he now knew was a smaller than usual house for this neighborhood because nobody with money would build on this cursed ground. But inside . . .

Angel shook his head. He had been inside the house before, and it had looked like a house, in spite of the carnage all over the place. Now, it was only house-like on the outside. Inside, it was something entirely different. At first glance, it resembled a vast cavern. But instead of stone, the walls were slick, as if some thick liquid coated them, running down the sides, dripping here and there to form viscous, fluid stalactites. It all glowed softly with some inner illumination. They were as pink, Angel noted with a shudder, as the inside of some giant maw.

And the stench was almost overwhelming. The

hot, humid air smelled like some gaseous pocket inside the earth's core had been breached, the fumes mingling with generational layers of rotting carcasses on the way to the surface.

Coming through the strange doorway, he still had been able to hear the calls of the police officers outside, ordering him to stop. Now that he was inside, their shouts, if they continued, were drowned out by the resumption of the sounds Angel had heard before, magnified a hundredfold, like noises under water. That metallic screech was nearly deafening, the howl of the wind, the moaning and sighing like a billion lost souls seeking refuge tore at him. Underneath it all, he heard a different sound, a kind of shuffling, scrabbling noise that grew steadily louder.

Or was it that? he wondered. *Steadily louder . . . or steadily closer?*

He gripped the sword as if it might offer him some protection, and wished he didn't have to find out which.

While Wesley finished up on the phone with Angel, Cordelia rapped on the door of Mac Lindley's mobile home. Wes wished she hadn't done that—he had wanted to have a last-minute consultation with the others before they made their presence known. *Too late now,* he reasoned. He folded his phone and returned it to his pocket, hoping that whatever Angel faced inside that house, he would be able to best it without too much difficulty.

He hoped the same of whatever they discovered here.

He caught up to the others at the doorway. Fred regarded him with her big brown eyes. "No one's answering," she said.

"Right. Well, he's probably in a soundproofed inner room," Wesley speculated. "He wouldn't want to just broadcast from the trailer—wouldn't want street noises to be picked up by the microphone."

Even as he said it, he realized that this spot was a long way from anything resembling civilization. There was probably the occasional car or truck passing by, and maybe the howl of a coyote or the hoot of an owl, but in fact this would be a relatively quiet place from which to broadcast.

Connor rapped on the door, harder than Cordelia had. "Lindley!" he shouted. "Open up!"

There was still no answer from inside. Wesley swallowed. They would have to break in. He didn't know what he expected to find in there, but somehow he didn't think it would be a jovial radio host eager to welcome visitors. Wes had left the car radio playing until he'd shut off the engine, and Mac Lindley's voice had sounded more and more odd, his words slurred, almost unintelligible. Not that they'd been especially clear before, at least, not since he'd launched into all-incantation, all the time. But still, there had been the occasional place-name or Latin word that Wesley had been able to make out. The last few minutes, however, Lindley might as well have been reading words backward, and from a Russian dictionary. Or a Klingon one.

"Give me some space," Connor said. "I'll open it."

"Connor, no!" Cordelia objected. "You're still hurt!"

Lorne caught Wesley's eye. "She's right, Connor," he said. "Let Wes do it."

"It's just an old trailer," Connor complained. "Anyway, I'm better."

"I'm sure you heal fast," Wesley argued. "But it would still be safer to allow me."

Connor shrugged. "Whatever," he said. "Do it your way."

Wesley stood back to let the others clear away from the door. But before she moved, Fred gave the knob a twist.

The door swung open.

From inside, a smell like a meat locker a month after the electricity had failed assailed their nostrils. Wesley put his hand over his nose and mouth. Fred gagged. Everyone made faces, except Lorne, who smiled broadly. "At least there's something that smells worse than I did the other night," he said cheerfully. "I was starting to think I'd set a new record."

"Glad you're happy about it," Connor groused.

Braving the stench, they all entered through the narrow doorway. Wesley went first, then Connor, Fred, and Cordelia. Lorne brought up the rear. Each carried the same weapon they had used in the battle earlier, except that Lorne had traded in his crossbow for a two-headed ax.

The mobile home looked just as Wesley had expected. The built-in furnishings were old and worn, all in earth tones. The cabinets were scarred, but whole. It looked as if Lindley lived there full-time. Wes led the way down the short hallway, toward a closed door. He guessed that Lindley was on the other side of the door, broadcasting his bizarre spell. He could hear a muffled drone that was probably Lindley's voice. "Through there," he suggested.

"I think so," Cordelia agreed.

"I can't believe I'm saying this," Lorne added, "but there's no time like the present."

Wesley nodded and put a hand on the knob to the interior door. He tried to steel himself for whatever might be on the other side: Mac Lindley aiming a gun at them, paranoid about intruders? More likely, he knew, Lindley with headphones on, completely unaware of their presence.

He turned the knob and tugged the door open.

On the other side of it, Lindley's broadcasting booth was primitive but functional. The door, walls, and ceiling were soundproofed with acoustical tiles. A console in the middle of the room held the equipment he needed, including a microphone on a tabletop stand, various tape players, gauges, dials, and dozens of buttons. In front of the console was a comfortable office chair, on wheels, the kind that someone could sit in for hours without having to leave it.

But sitting in the chair was no Mac Lindley.

A figure was there, to be sure. Its mouth was moving, and the incantation came out of it. But the words being spoken now were not words that any human mouth had ever voiced, or ever could. And though the figure in the chair looked as if it might once have been human, it wasn't now.

A checkered shirt and blue jeans littered the floor at the base of the chair, shredded as if they had split and fallen off when the body at the console had swollen to twice human size. The exposed flesh was a purplish green, a sickly color that reminded Wesley of spoiled fruit. It bulged and swelled in places humans didn't, and it rippled as Wes watched, as if there was something squirming about underneath it. Wesley felt sick to his stomach, looking at the abomination before him. He heard various responses from his friends, from a low whistle to a retching noise.

The thing that had been Mac Lindley lifted its head slowly, as if to look at them, crowding in the doorway. When it did, Wesley realized that even though its mouth still moved in imitation of humanity, and words issued from it, its eyeballs— Mac's eyeballs, at any rate—were gone. The thing regarded them with empty sockets. As Wesley watched, its forehead bulged and then flattened again, very much as if a fist had been pushed against the flesh there from the inside.

"Somehow, *ick* just doesn't do it justice," Cordelia whispered.

"Not even close," Lorne agreed.

Wes raised a hand to shush them. "Mr. Lindley," he tried. "Are you . . . in there?"

The not-Mac just continued uttering syllables that sounded meaningless but no doubt were not.

"What happened to him?" Fred asked.

"I can only speculate," Wesley replied softly. "But if I were to do so, I would remind you of the story Gunn told us."

"Oh, about the male and female demons, or gods or whatever they were?"

"Right," Wesley said. "The male, according to the story, is coming back to Earth via the Fletcher house. I daresay Angel is probably there right now, facing it down. But we—"

"What?" Connor interrupted. "What does it have to do with old Mac here?"

"I think he died and his body's trapped gases are bloating him," Fred said.

"It's much worse than that, Fred," Wesley said. "I'm sure Mac is dead. But he's not just a victim, he's a vessel."

"I think I see what you're getting at, Wes," Lorne put in. "And Cordy's right: *Ick* doesn't even begin to cover it."

"What?" Connor asked.

"Well," Wes explained, "if the male is returning inside the Fletcher house, the female has to come back someplace as well. And it's my guess that she's doing so right here, in front of us. The goddess is using Lindley's body as her transfer point— emerging into our world through him."

"And using him to transmit the incantation that returns her lover," Cordelia added.

"Very elegant, in a disgusting sort of way," Lorne observed.

"I suspect there's even more to it," Wes said. The thought had just now occurred to him, but it seemed to make sense. "I think this is the reason Mac started his 'monster cleanup' campaign."

"What is?" Fred wanted to know. "The female doesn't want her boyfriend tempted by vampires and demons?"

"No, not exactly," Wesley replied. "I suspect she doesn't want any creatures around powerful enough to challenge them. When they both return to Earth, they want to be the strongest things around. They want to rule, and to not have to worry about anyone else banishing them again. By reducing L.A. down to just its human population, and them, they'd be safe here."

"I think you're right," Cordelia said. "They were in love, and remember, Gunn said they had created the natural beauty of the area—at least according to the legend. Now that they're back, they don't want anyone to challenge them. And they'll try to restore the 'beauty' to the way they like it. Which, if Mac here is any indication, isn't going to be popular with the *InStyle* crowd."

"So what can we do to stop it?" Connor wondered.

"That," Wesley said, "is what we need to figure out. And quickly."

CHAPTER EIGHTEEN

Weary and battered, sword in hand, Angel searched the—*well, house,* he thought, *doesn't seem to be the right word anymore*—looking for the source of the strange noises, or any other indication of what had transformed this place, and why.

The rules of physics seemed to have gone awry. The outside of the place had seemed the same size that it was on his first visit, but on the inside, it was vast and many-chambered, with—for lack of a better description—grotto after grotto, all formed of the same viscous goo, dripping from ceilings and flowing down walls like slow, cool lava. With the exception of the sounds he had heard since arriving, everything else seemed to be silent—his own footfalls, on the slightly tacky floor, made no sound, and neither did the drips and globs falling around him.

Angel didn't know exactly where he was going or what to expect when he got there. One direction looked the same as another, and the noises resonated throughout the whole place more or less equally. He had the impression that the shuffling sound was getting closer, but closer to where? With no landmarks, he had completely lost his bearings.

Finally, Angel had had enough. The frustrations of the past couple of nights came rushing to the fore, the rage within him swelled, and he jammed the point of the sword down as hard as he could into the floor. "Where are you?!" he shouted at the top of his lungs. "What are you? What do you want?"

Instead of echoing, the soft chambers absorbed his voice almost instantly, so even to his own ears, it sounded muffled. But after a second, he heard another voice.

"Help! Whoever you are, call again so we can find you!"

The near panic in the voice was evident, but so was the humanity. Angel was astonished to hear that there were humans in there. *The cops outside,* he realized suddenly. Some of them must have come in before the house sealed itself off and transformed itself. "I'm here!" Angel called back. "Come to my voice!"

"Keep talking!" the other voice returned, coming closer.

Angel knew that staying put was the best course. If he went searching for them while they looked for him, they'd be as likely to miss one another as to meet. "I'll get you out!" he shouted. "I'm . . . I can't describe where I am, it all looks alike!"

Then he saw movement, coming from one of the half-dozen entry points into the chamber he had stopped in. "Right here!" he called.

"Oh, thank God!" A female voice. Angel watched the entry, sword at the ready in case it was all some kind of trick. Two uniformed police officers rushed toward him. Their uniforms were askew, shirts untucked and soiled. She was young, pretty, and fit, but the man looked like he stretched the police department's maximum-weight requirement to the limit. Both were wild-eyed with terror, but the woman offered a weak smile when she looked at Angel. "You are a man, right?" she asked. "Not some kind of mirage?"

"Yes," Angel lied. *Close enough, anyway.* "How long have you been in here?"

The man shrugged, smacking the watch at his wrist. "Our watches stopped right after we came in," he explained. "Right when the doors went away. Radios and phones too."

"Can you get us out?" the woman queried anxiously. "You said you could."

"I think so," Angel answered. He remembered Wesley's spell to come in—he just wasn't one-hundred-percent sure it would work without knowing where there was a doorway or window to pass through.

"You think?!" the male officer echoed angrily. "You got in here, didn't you? You must know a way out!"

"It's not that easy," Angel pointed out. "Obviously a lot of the regular rules don't apply here."

"You can say that again," the woman confirmed. "Place has been changing ever since we got in here."

"Give me a minute and I'll see what I can do," Angel promised. He turned away from the police officers—mostly because, in spite of its effectiveness, he felt a little silly reciting a spell in front of them—and spoke the words Wes had taught him.

For a horrible few seconds, nothing happened. But then—almost grudgingly, it seemed—a few spots on the chamber's wall took on the familiar, semitranslucent, gelatinous cast. "Hurry!" Angel urged. "I don't know how long they'll last."

"What are they?" the male cop asked.

"They're doorways." Even as he said it, Angel realized he wasn't entirely sure where they would lead, or where in the house they might be. They could be in for an unpleasant surprise when they threw themselves through the doorway if they happened to be in the basement.

But that was all the cops had to hear. They rushed the closest one and charged through it, obviously more than ready to be finished with this whole horrific experience. Angel followed and was relieved, once he had passed through, to see that they were in the front of the house, on the ground level. The other police officers rushed toward them as soon as they emerged.

The male cop started toward his buddies, but Angel was able to grab the woman's shoulder before she moved away. "Listen," he said. "I just want to hear what you saw while you were in there. Was there any indication of what is behind all this?"

She shook her head. "We saw these bodies—horrible murders. But then the doors and windows vanished, and we started looking for a way out. As we did, the rest of the house started to change—like you saw it. Only first it was more liquid, like the whole house melted into this other, strange shape. Finally, it started to harden. That's been going on for a while now."

"What about the bodies?" Angel demanded. "Where are they now?"

"I don't know," she said, shaking her head. "They disappeared somehow, when the house changed. How long were we in there?"

"Not that long, I don't think," Angel said. "A few hours, maybe."

"Seems like days," she said. There was a haunted look in her eyes. "Who are you, anyway?"

Angel ignored the question and looked back toward the house. The doorways were still visible, but he didn't think they would be for long. He liked the cool night air on his skin, and the idea of going back into that steamy, stinking, oozing place filled him with dread.

But he knew that was exactly why he needed to do it. With a last glance at the female police officer, he ran back toward the house and passed through the doorway.

Even in the few moments he had been outside, the place had continued to change. The walls and floor had hardened, as the cop had described, taking on the texture of rock now instead of a semigelatinous liquid. The color hadn't changed, but now it reminded Angel of the salmon color that some desert landscapes have, except for the soft internal glow cast by the walls.

The sounds and smells, if anything, had increased. Angel thought he understood what at least some of the noises were. This place was changing, transforming in some incredible way. A change like that—even a magickal one—probably came with a certain amount of noise as the very atoms were rearranged into some other shape and substance. Every house creaked a little, just from settling, but this one was going through a much more major experience, and the noises were louder too.

That didn't explain the smells, though, or the underlying noise that sounded ever closer. He had his own theory about that, too. If he was right, then the story Gunn had told Fred was much more than just a legend.

He held up the sword in his hand, which seemed very slender and frail just now. If he was right, he'd need a much bigger sword.

"Are you okay, Julia? What happened in there?" Marilyn Olsson brought a blanket from her squad car and wrapped it around Julia's shoulders. Marilyn was her best friend in the precinct, an older blond woman who had been through just about everything but still kept her grace and good humor.

"That's a little hard to say, Marilyn," Julia replied. She knew she'd have to talk about it sometime, but for the moment she wasn't sure how, didn't even have the vocabulary to describe what she and Ron had experienced. She looked around. There were four other cars parked outside. No press, and no brass, for which she was grateful. "Looks like you kept a lid on this," she speculated.

"We didn't know what we were keeping a lid on," Marilyn said. "The city's a madhouse tonight, stuff going on everywhere. Once a few of us got here and discovered that—well, we didn't know what had happened, but you were inside and we couldn't get in—we made a cell call to the captain and told him we didn't want any radio chatter on it. Didn't want a bunch of reporters here getting in our way. Captain had plenty on his mind, so he didn't argue. And then we've just been waiting here. That guy showed up a little while ago and went inside before we could stop him."

"It's a good thing he did," Julia said. "Or we'd still be in there."

Marilyn led Julia over to where the rest of the cops had gathered around Ron, who was less hesitant to try to describe what he'd seen. ". . . like bubble gum," he was saying, "or maybe taffy. Pink taffy. And the stench—man, you couldn't believe the smell."

Kevin Blaine strode over toward them from his squad car. "I've called in that guy's tag," he said. "Car's not even registered. They're checking farther back to see if it's ever been."

"Don't—" Julia began.

"Don't what? You don't want to know who that clown is?"

"It's just . . . I have a feeling about him," she said. For the second time in minutes, she found herself having a hard time putting her feelings into words. "I don't know who he is or what he's doing, but . . . he went back *in* there, you know? I mean, maybe it doesn't mean so much to you guys because you haven't been inside. But anyone who would do that willingly . . . I just think maybe we owe it to him to hold off."

Ron started to say something—to object, Julia guessed, or to exaggerate his own role in what had happened. She figured he would be doing so with great regularity in the days and weeks to come. He'd have the war story to top all war stories. She realized that she was bothered by that—that if the topic of this house, this night, never came up again, she would be happy. She didn't like things she couldn't explain, things that threatened her worldview. This definitely fell into that category.

Ron read her look and clamped his mouth shut. A couple of the other officers started to reply, but Julia was adamant. Since she and Ron were the ones who had been inside, the others decided to bow to their wishes. But they would wait until the guy came out again, and question him then. Kevin Blaine insisted on that, and Julia didn't argue the point.

She wouldn't mind getting a chance to talk with the stranger again herself.

Gunn knew the hotel would be empty when he got there. Fred was on the road with Cordy, Connor, Lorne, and Wes. He had checked in with them a couple of times by phone, but knew that if he kept calling, he'd be a pest instead of a concerned friend. And Angel was on his way back up to the

Fletcher place. Gunn was too far out to reach either party in time to do any good, given the way the city was tonight. *More of a war zone than a laid-back California wonderland.*

Getting to the hotel had been a challenge. There had been roads blocked off, cars and buildings in flames, armed groups of people roaming the streets. Gunn figured everything was finally coming to a head, and by the time the sun set again, things would have calmed down—at least, he desperately hoped so. He didn't like Fred being out there on such a dangerous night without him around to protect her.

Fred. He sniffed the air near the desk she usually used and caught traces of her scent. He figured he was acting like a lovesick kid. But there was no one around to know about it, so he didn't care. He had learned some hard lessons about life in the last couple of years, and one was that if you love someone, you are opening yourself up to a lot of sorrow and heartbreak. Maybe the old saying isn't true—you don't always hurt the one you love, but it is apparently hard to love without getting hurt.

Alonna had not intentionally hurt him, but having to drive a stake into the only family he had left in the world had caused a scar on his heart that would never heal. Falling in love with Fred had taken an act of courage that, as far as he was concerned, was greater than that required to walk alone and unarmed into a nest of hungry vamps.

But he had done it willingly because she was worth it.

Now he had lost her. He was increasingly convinced he'd lost her for good, all because he had tried to do the right thing by her. She was out there with Wesley, who had always been competition for her, always had an eye for her, and he was here alone in the marble-floored lobby of the Hyperion Hotel while outside, the city, *his* city, cried out in mortal pain.

Gunn shook his head. He would love a solid eight hours of shut-eye. But it wasn't happening tonight.

He went back out into the city.

CHAPTER NINETEEN

As Angel walked through what had clearly become caverns, he was able to pinpoint the location of the loud, scrabbling noise. Somehow as the fleshy walls and floor hardened, the groaning noises subsided and the other one, the one that seemed to be getting closer and closer, took precedence. It sounded like thousands of claws scrabbling over rock.

He knew what he thought it was. He thought it was the male god, returning to the surface after a long banishment. Looking for his mate.

If he was right, he also knew that it was best met head-on. Since the surfaces were of a more familiar material and the directional signals of sounds seemed to be working again, he headed toward the source of the strange noise. He passed through one chamber after another, the walls pitted and with holes and, in some cases, still seeping trace bits of fluid, but for the most part as hard as if someone had taken the building and fired it in a kiln.

As he got closer to the source of the sound, the stench grew worse as well, turning his stomach. But he had no choice. This thing was emerging into his city, and he was the only one who could fight it.

He knew he was close when clouds of steam started to clog the air. He pushed on, disregarding the smell, the aches that plagued him, the tiny, niggling doubt that said, *You can't do this. This is too big, even for you.* He *had* to do this. His son's life could depend on it. The lives of his friends.

Who knew what havoc the god could wreak on Los Angeles if his mere approach had such a powerful impact?

He pushed on, through the steam. Sweat rolled down him in waves as the superheated air pounded him. Finally, he saw a different kind of glow rippling on the walls—a reflected one rather than the now-familiar internal.

Another chamber, this one with ceilings low enough to touch. Here, the glow was more pronounced, the heat almost unbearable. Angel pressed on.

The oppressive chamber opened into another that was impossibly vast. The room would have taken more space than the entire Fletcher property. Angel guessed that it was fifty yards across, almost perfectly circular. The ceiling was at least thirty yards over his head.

In the middle of the room was a massive hole.

The hole was probably forty feet in diameter. Magma bubbled and boiled from it, spitting toward Angel in fiery globs. The scrambling sounds were loud, almost deafening.

Whatever was coming wasn't far off.

Angel braced himself to look over the edge of the hole. No way to guess what he might see. And he didn't know how close it was, didn't know if it might attack the instant he showed himself.

All his aches and pains, all his weariness, was forgotten now. He had to be ready for anything.

He was almost close enough to look in when he saw the hand appear at the edge of the hole.

Mac Lindley, or the thing that had once been him, showed no reaction to their visit, as far as Connor could see. He—or it—kept on rambling into the microphone, not even noticing them as they gathered around it. Connor was afraid Fred, consumed with scientific curiosity, was going to poke the big ugly, which worried him because it looked like something that might burst like a swollen blister.

"What do you think we should do?" Fred asked.

At least she lowered her finger instead of touching the Lindley-thing. Small comfort.

"Do?" Connor echoed. "We should kill it!"

"I'm not sure that's wise," Wesley countered. "Perhaps there's a way we can use her to reverse the incantation."

"She doesn't look like she's in any mood for negotiation," Lorne pointed out. "I'm not sure she even knows we're here."

"She knows," Cordelia stated.

Connor wondered how Cordy could know something like that. But then again, she had been a higher being. Maybe that had left her with a better understanding of all sorts of other beings: higher, lower, and unpleasant. He knew where he stood— kill it fast, before it did anything nasty. He would just go for it, but the way Wes had jumped down his throat when he had mentioned it made him hold off. Wesley was a smart guy, there was no denying that, and he had a lot of experience, even if he could be tricked out of a baby from time to time.

Still, as it sat there blabbing into the microphone, its flesh puckering and bubbling like pizza cheese in an oven, all Connor could think of was how much he wanted it dead.

The hand was small, smaller than Angel's own, not the kind of hand he would associate with a god. It was joined momentarily by a second one and then a head—round, bald, with the standard two eyes, a nose and a mouth, but flat-featured, with wide, narrow eyes, mere nostril flaps for a nose, a grin full of jagged teeth, and ears that flopped over and ended in points. It was almost comical, except for the way it fixed Angel with a glare that looked like pure hatred.

Then more hands showed up—a dozen, two— and more heads, and then they charged from the hole, their pale skinny bodies naked but armed with long, razorlike claws at the ends of their tapered fingers and toes. A river of them spilled from the hole. They ran at Angel with fury in their eyes, strange keening noises erupting from their throats.

He didn't know who they were, but their intent was obvious. He backed up against one of the now-solid rock walls so they couldn't surround him, and waited for the first wave to get into range of his sword. Then he slashed with all the strength he could muster.

The creatures didn't seem to know fear. They clambered over their own dead, jabbing clawed hands toward him, their bizarre war cry never fading until they died. He sliced right and left, chopping through them, and their thin frames offered little resistance. But the sight of their fellows losing limbs and heads, being split down the middle, spurting thick blue blood with every swing of the blade, didn't slow them down for an instant.

Still, they came, crawling from the hole and heading instantly toward the battle. Angel wondered how long he could keep up the slaughter. His arm, already tired, began to hurt. The sword seemed almost impossibly heavy. There were so many of them, he couldn't possibly keep them all at bay. Sharp nails ripped his clothes, raked his flesh. He thought his eardrums would rupture from the sound of their cries.

But he knew he couldn't give up. This demonic army must be advance troops paving the way for their god's approach. If he defeated them, maybe their master would get the idea that he wasn't wanted and would go back where he came from.

Then again, Angel remembered, *where he came from is here.*

He raised the sword again, and fought.

And finally, the river dried up. Nothing more came from the hole except steam and heat. Even the magma had stopped flowing now. Angel took a deep breath and allowed himself a few moments to sit on the ground and gather his strength. He looked around and tried to estimate the number of demonic bodies in the chamber with him, but it was no use. They were in too many pieces. *A hundred, at least,* he guessed. *Probably more.*

The chamber was finally quiet. No more scrabbling sounds from the hole. No more wailing demons. Maybe it had been them all along, clawing their way to the surface. Maybe they *were* the god, or a manifestation of him. Maybe that was it, and the battle was done.

Yeah, he thought, *and monkeys might fly out of . . . never mind. Just don't get greedy. You'll be done when it's over, not before.*

After a brief respite, he pushed off the wall, back to his feet, and stepped over the carnage toward the hole. This time, no hands appeared, and he leaned over it and looked down. It was a long tunnel, as straight as an elevator shaft.

And there was something in it, something enormous.

The god had arrived.

Wesley folded the phone and angrily stuck it back into his pocket. "I wish we could reach Angel," he said. "I'd like to know that whatever we do here doesn't have some sort of fallout for him that we're not taking into account."

"Yeah, I'm with you, nutmeg," Lorne agreed, scratching the base of his right horn. "But you know him and cell phones. I guess we'll have to wing it. Got any brilliant ideas?"

Wes considered for a moment. "I don't know about brilliant," he said. "But perhaps we can still offer a counter-spell that will stop the return of these two beings in their tracks."

"By using the radio broadcast, the same way Lindley did," Fred added. "If enough people still have their radios on, then . . ."

"Precisely," Wes said with satisfaction. "If we believe that her incantation was effective because there were so many radios broadcasting it, so many listeners hearing the words that Mac was speaking, then it's quite possible that by utilizing the same mechanism, we might just be able to stop everything before it's too late."

"Or we could just kill it," Connor suggested again. "And be done with it."

Wesley shook his head. "I suspect that would be more difficult than you think, Connor."

"But you don't know for sure until you try."

Wesley glanced pleadingly at Cordelia. "Let's try it Wes's way first, Connor," she said. "And if it doesn't work, then we try your way."

Connor didn't listen to many people, but he listened to Cordelia, for which Wes was grateful. Connor shrugged. "Whatever."

"You do have a spell in mind—right, Wesley?" Fred inquired. She ticked her gaze toward Mac Lindley's body, which was swelling again, enveloping its whole chair in the folds of its mutating flesh. "Because if you have to make one up, I'm not sure we have time."

That is *a problem,* Wesley thought. He didn't want to unduly alarm the others, but the fact was, the goddess's incantation had been completely unfamiliar to him. She wasn't using any of the standard magickal systems, which made sense because a being of her level of power would certainly have a system all her own. But that meant that a counter-spell wouldn't be found in any handy grimoire or mystical library. It would, in fact, have to be either crafted from scratch or adapted from some existing spell.

"Let me just listen for a few moments," he said, holding up a hand for silence. Everyone quieted. The mouth that had once been Mac Lindley's had been speaking the whole time, though it twisted and curled into shapes that no human mouth could make as it spoke words never meant for Earthly tongues.

". . . konoth shia shulamon distiera ia ia nester-i from Fernbush glissentriad ia from Nimes. Tekeli-li ista ia from Parkwood from Rosebush from Oak Tree ia kosterdom sluggoth tideren shiai mallota."

"Oak Tree," Fred repeated in an urgent whisper. "That's the street that Angel said the Fletcher house is on."

"Yes," Wesley agreed. "All those names are of streets in that immediate vicinity. I believe that means her male counterpart is getting closer to surfacing—we've got to act quickly if we're going to stop it."

"Do you have a spell in mind?" Cordelia asked.

"I'm getting there," Wesley said. "I just need a few minutes."

As if in answer, the body of Mac Lindley bubbled and expanded once again, his arms drooping onto the floor. His mouth kept up its constant stream of babble.

"Those better be the shortest minutes in history," Lorne said. "Because I think we're fresh out of time."

CHAPTER TWENTY

It was huge, and it was horrible. Those were Angel's first two reactions to the sight of the god slithering up its tunnel toward the surface.

Violence is never pretty, he thought. *And while this thing may not mean to commit violence, plenty has already been done just by its approach. If it comes back to Earth, there's no telling how many more might die. The god may not be evil, per se, but by trying to reclaim something that is no longer his, he is doing evil. And he needs to be stopped, here and now.*

He steeled himself to look once more into the pit.

It was coming ever closer—just fifty feet away, if that—and he could see it in more detail, illuminated by the soft glow from inside the pit walls. Although he couldn't tell how far down the tunnel it stretched, it seemed to be basically wormlike in shape, a long cylinder of flesh and muscle. Angel had no real frame of reference, just a guess as to how close it really was, but he guessed that the god was about a dozen feet in diameter.

The end that was coming toward Angel was obviously its head. Two black, incurious eyes stared straight ahead, but Angel couldn't tell if it saw anything at all. It might well have been blind from its many centuries under the earth. The eyes were big and round, the size of a dinner plate, almost all dark pupils, with just a little bloodshot white visible around the outer rims. There were no eyelids he could make out, and bits of dirt and debris from the tunnel floated on their liquid surface.

Beneath the eyes were what seemed to be several flapped openings that he took to be breathing apparatus of some kind, a nose or a gill. They fluttered as if air passed through, in on one side and then a moment later out on the other.

And below that was the part that really worried Angel: a mouth that was at least six feet across—if his estimation was correct. The mouth was slightly parted, and inside it, Angel could see teeth that seemed as big as short swords, glistening with thick, viscous saliva that drooled down the thing's sides as if to lubricate its passage out of the pit.

Its flesh was pale white, like that of the heralds, almost transparent—Angel thought he could see veins and even organs under its surface—and uneven, with hundreds of bumps and nodules and blisters that he could make out just on its face and head. There were also stray hairs emerging in clumps from various parts of its face—thick as ropes and long, trailing behind it beyond the point that Angel could see.

The god must have had a thousand legs, or more—ill-defined stalks that jutted out from its body in every direction. These were what slowly propelled it up from the pit as they reached out to the pit walls and pushed. They couldn't have been more than a few inches long, he thought. They would not be the danger, if the thing were allowed to emerge. Its mouth was the problem. It could easily swallow him whole.

He felt a little sorry for the god, in an offhand way. He sympathized, at least, with its goal. His own existence had been an endless ballet of love and death, although he suspected the same was true of most everyone else on the planet. Love and loss, he had learned, are closely linked. Maybe a wise person would give up the search for the former in order to avoid facing the latter again and again. But Angel wasn't that wise. Or else he wasn't willing to skip on the love part, however fleeting, for fear of the pain that might follow.

Even so, he wasn't going to show it any mercy. Its time here had come and gone.

He determined that the thing would be easiest to kill before it got out of the pit. The eyes, huge and round, were probably vulnerable points. No way to tell where its brain was, if it even had one, but the usual rule in the animal kingdom was that the brain was close to the eyes, so that was worth a try. The only hard part would be getting to the eyes without getting in range of the mouth. Angel wished that he had brought a crossbow or a spear in with him instead of a sword.

He looked around the chamber for something he might use as a weapon. Most of the floor was covered with dead heralds, and their only weapons were their own claws. The place seemed like it should be rocky, but the way it had been formed, all the surface irregularities were fused to the walls and floor, not separate pieces. Angel shoved a few of the carcasses aside and grabbed at an upthrust chunk the size of a small boulder. He tugged and pulled, even tried shoving the blade of his sword underneath to pry the thing up. It wouldn't budge. It might as well have been cemented down with the strongest mortar ever invented. In frustration, Angel kicked at it with a booted foot. *No use*, he thought. *It's not going to break off.*

He glanced back down the pit. The god was even closer—and it looked bigger than it had before. Its progress was slow, but steady.

If there was nothing loose in the cavern except

dead soldiers, Angel decided, he might as well start with those. Maybe their claws would at least cause the god some pain, convince it that this whole incursion was a bad idea. He lifted one over his head, carried it to the rim, and hurled it down at the approaching god with all his strength. The body slammed into the unclosing eye and bounced. Angel thought the god's progress might have been minutely slowed, but he wasn't sure. He went back for another corpse, and threw it after the first.

This time, when the body landed closer to the nose flaps, the god's mouth opened as much as the pit's circumference would allow, and a long, blue-white tongue licked out, curling around the herald's carcass like a prehensile tail. The tongue rolled the body toward the open maw and then popped it in, as if swallowing a treat.

And still, the god came.

Feeling the almost unbearable pressure of the situation, Wesley nevertheless knew that he had to take a few moments to compose his thoughts. He found some paper on Mac's desk and sat on the floor in a corner of the trailer, scribbling down notes on a spell that he thought might work. He knew it was probably too late to bar the approach of the gods. But they hadn't emerged yet, so closing off the portals they hoped to use might still be possible. It seemed the best bet, anyway.

There were a variety of portal-closing spells he knew. The most efficient was probably an ancient Etruscan one that he had used a couple of times in the past. A problem with the Etruscan spell might be that it very specifically referred to a single portal, and in this case it seemed he needed to deal with two different portals, in two different places, that most likely needed to be shut simultaneously. If either god broke free into this world, then the problems of the last few days would seem minor by comparison. And Wes didn't even know precisely what the portal the male god was using might be like. Possibly it was utilizing the body of Herman Fletcher or one of his family, the way this one was using Mac Lindley. But then again, none of those bodies were still alive, so Wesley figured that was only a 50 percent or less probability.

He feared any attempt was doomed to failure, or only partial success at best.

On the bright side, he knew Angel was at the other portal. If it had been anyone else, Wesley would have despaired. But Angel was—well, he was Angel. If anyone could stop a god in its tracks, Angel was the guy.

A wet popping sound came from the other side of the booth, accompanied by sounds of surprise from Wesley's friends. "Umm, Wes, I think you'd better hurry up with that spell," Cordelia called.

"Coming," Wesley replied. He rose and brought the paper with him. When he approached, he saw what the noise had been—half of Mac's head had fallen away, and a yellow-green tentacle was wiggling out through the opening. On its underside were round suckers with barbed, hook-like appendages in their centers. "Oh."

"Yeah, 'oh' is a good word for it," Lorne offered. "But then again, so is, 'we need to do something, and fast.'"

"Connor," Wes instructed, "we need that microphone. Can you reach it?"

Connor moved instantly to the console. The microphone was on a stand, not built in, which at least was one point in their favor. Lindley's body had swollen so much that no one could simply reach around it to take the microphone away, but Connor leaped to the top of the console, leaned down, and scooped it up. He was about to carry it off when the tentacle emerging from Lindley's body shot out and wrapped around Connor's wrist.

"Ow!" he shouted, his face twisting in pain. Wesley guessed that the hooks within each sucker had already inserted themselves into Connor's flesh, and the more he pulled to get his arm out of its grip, the more the barbs would tear at him. With his free hand, Connor snatched his dagger from his belt and sliced at the tentacle. The blade sank deep into the thing's flesh, and the tentacle jerked away, curling in on itself. At the same time, Mac Lindley's right arm tore off his body at the shoulder, and the wriggling tip of another tentacle appeared.

Connor jumped back to the floor, holding the microphone. His wrist bled from several spots and was already purpling where the thing had held him. "That monster's got a grip!" he announced.

"We need to put the kibosh on it before it goes all giant squid on the rest of us," Lorne said anxiously.

"That's the idea," Wesley said. "I've got a spell, but I need to be able to compose as I go, so I don't want to be the one speaking into the microphone—"

Cordelia's hand shot into the air. "Pick me, pick me!" she said. "I always wanted my own radio show. Well, I mean, I thought it would be a fun sideline after I was a movie star."

"That's fine, Cordelia," Wesley agreed. "You just have to repeat everything I tell you, exactly as I say it. No improvising."

"I'm script girl," Cordelia promised. "Not improv girl. I swear."

"Very well." Connor handed Cordelia the microphone. She carried it as far away from the console as its cord would allow. Wesley knew they had to move fast now, before more tentacles emerged. If the goddess managed to shut down the console, they were lost.

He glanced down at his notes and then turned to Cordelia. "Repeat precisely what I tell you to, while I'm looking at you," he explained. "But if I look away from you and say anything, then I'm just composing what I want you to say. Got that?"

"Got it, Wes."

"Very well," he said. "Let's go. No, don't say that. I'll signal with my finger when you begin."

"Can I do a station ID first?" she asked.

"No." He gathered his thoughts for a second, then looked right into Cordelia's brown eyes and wagged a finger at her. "O portalis ex cammandia brist nocolature," he recited. He paused, and Cordelia repeated it syllable for syllable. "No portal shall exist here, no doorway through which to pass," he said.

"Oh thank God, English," Lorne breathed.

"Shhh!" Wesley cautioned. He didn't want the microphone picking up any extraneous sounds.

Cordelia repeated the phrase, and Wesley continued, in ancient Etruscan again. He figured that alternating between the lost language and English would mean listeners were more likely to leave their radios on. If they had stayed tuned in through Mac's inhuman gibberish, he suspected that they would probably listen in while Cordy recited her part.

"Kolandis ignostum portalis striend," he said. Cordy arched an eyebrow at him but repeated it flawlessly.

"The portal closes imminently," he went on.

"The portal closes imminently," Cordelia said with a smile. Clearly, she liked the English part best.

Just as clearly, the goddess didn't like any of it. Mac Lindley's body shuddered, and the remaining part of his head split open with a hiss of escaping fumes as another tentacle burst free. All three of them stretched toward Cordelia, who looked at Wesley with an uneasy grin. "Hurry up," she mouthed silently.

CHAPTER TWENTY-ONE

The god was finally close enough for Angel to get a true sense of its size. Where he had thought it was perhaps a dozen feet in diameter, he realized it was actually closer to twenty. Which meant that the mouth with all the teeth in it, and that awful prehensile tongue, was more like ten. He wouldn't be much more than a bonbon to it.

The foul stench of it rose from the pit like a tidal wave, like the rush of hot air ahead of a subway train.

The bodies of its soldiers didn't slow it at all. And there was nothing else here to use. Angel wished he'd thought to bring some dynamite along, but that was a bit outside of his usual operating procedure. Maybe he needed something like Batman's utility belt—surely the Caped Crusader would at least have some handy Bat-grenades in there.

He knew he couldn't just leave. Even taking the time to go outside and look for something he might be able to use against it—the cops outside had shotguns, and maybe grenades of their own—could give it enough time to get out of the pit. He was afraid that once it was out, his last advantage would be gone. While it was confined within the space of the pit, it didn't have much freedom of movement. Once it was out, however, it would have size, strength, and maybe speed in its favor. He had to stop it inside the pit.

Somehow.

Using only a sword and his own exhausted, aching muscles.

Part of Angel had hoped that when he finally expired, it would be with Cordy at his side. *Guess that's not going to happen*, he thought. He wasn't giving up, but he figured his chances weren't good enough that he'd be able to defeat this thing. And while vampires were tough to kill—again—this looked like just the sort of beast that might be able to pull it off without even breaking a sweat.

Angel braced himself as best he could at the edge of the pit, watching it lunge inexorably toward him. The closer it got, the faster he realized it was coming. He held the sword's hilt in both hands and raised it high above his head, point down. As soon as it was close enough, he planned to drive it into the god's eye and he hoped to follow through into its brain, stopping it instantly. If that didn't work, he was in some serious trouble. He was convinced there wouldn't be a second chance.

He held his ground as it neared. Even from a distance its hot, fetid breath assaulted his nostrils as if it were laced with acid. Its teeth clicked together, bluish tongue flicking against them as if in anticipation of a tasty snack. The thousands of stalk-like arms moved in a clockwork symmetry, pushing the god ever closer. Two dozen feet. A dozen. Ten.

At eight, Angel understood his mistake.

If he waited until he could reach the thing from here, it would be too late. Even if it died almost at once, it would at least have begun to emerge from the pit. And if it didn't die immediately, his only advantage would be gone. He had to stop it while it was still wholly within the pit.

He had to get down there with it.

Six feet.

Angel left the safety of the ground and jumped down onto it.

As he landed on its onrushing head, he drove the point of the sword down into the center of one of its massive eyes. A thin, fluid-filled membrane covered the pupil itself. That membrane burst when Angel stabbed into it and fluid gushed out and onto the surface of the god's face. The sword point drove down, and down, as Angel forced it through various levels of resistance. There were nerves somewhere inside it—the god didn't seem to slow in its advance, but its mouth opened, and a wail like a hundred sirens issued from it. That was the first noise it had made by itself, and Angel hoped it would be the last.

In spite of whatever pain he had caused, though, he hadn't stopped it. The thing burst from the mouth of the tunnel, throwing Angel off it. He bounced off a far wall and fell to the hard ground, stunned for a second. When he had gathered his senses and regained his feet—the sword had remained clutched in his fist the whole time—he saw something that had been concealed by the pit until now.

Dozens of long tentacles reached for him, each with saucer-size suckers from which barbed hooks protruded. Even as they did, the god opened its vast mouth and gnashed its teeth, sticky strings of saliva spanning the two rows.

Angel figured the god had gone a long time without a meal. The bodies he'd thrown at it had probably only whetted its appetite.

He was to be the main course.

"Hakatu klia weyndosh portalis meata." Cordelia repeated carefully. She wished Wesley had stuck to English—making her radio debut speaking a language that no one alive understood, outside of

Wesley and maybe a few other Watchers. *Giles,* she thought suddenly. *If Rupert Giles is listening somewhere, he'll appreciate my fluency.*

"A portal once opened must be shut," Wesley said. Cordelia repeated faithfully. The English was so much easier.

But she and Wes had to keep moving back, because Mac's tentacles—okay, the goddess's tentacles, she corrected herself—kept getting closer and closer. The microphone's cord was stretched to its absolute limit, and Connor, Fred, and Lorne used bladed weapons to try to keep the tentacles at bay. But there were more all the time now—Mac Lindley's body wasn't much more than a few ribbons of flesh holding the goddess in no more effectively than a thong on a sumo wrestler.

"A kanda wellishtin portalis durect," Wesley pronounced.

Cordelia repeated the phrase, her voice shaking a little as she tried to dodge a tentacle. Connor sliced at it, cutting into it, and it withdrew.

"Just a little longer," Wes whispered, looking away from Cordy so she wouldn't repeat it. Then, catching her gaze, he said, "The closing of the portal bars the way."

"Can I kill it now?" Connor pleaded. Instantly, Lorne, Fred, and Wesley all shushed him. But Cordelia was starting to come around to Connor's way of thinking. The less that remained of Mac

Lindley, the less reason there seemed to be to let the goddess live. And she wasn't helping with the counter-spell, merely hindering. Cordy couldn't quite find a downside to killing her.

Except, of course, that they might *not* be able to kill her. And that the trying might simply make her mad. Cordy spoke Wesley's words, wishing that they'd just hurry up and work already.

"The closing of the portal bars the way."

Cordelia's voice came from the speakers of a stereo inside a red BMW in Culver City. It issued from a radio on a kitchen countertop in Canoga Park as Sallie Cushman, the lady of the house, made an early breakfast. It came from speakers all over a bakery plant in Reseda, a twenty-four-hour drugstore in Inglewood, and a dry cleaners in Alhambra.

Outside the Los Angeles area, radio waves carried her voice to San Diego, to Bakersfield, to Lodi, to Monterey. Even farther away, Cordelia was heard in Joplin, in Nashville, in Des Moines and Madison and Utica and Key West. Everyplace there was a radio in North America that had been tuned to the Night Country, Cordelia's voice was heard.

It didn't even matter if anyone was listening. A magickal field had been established by Lindley's incantation, but under Cordelia's voice, that field warped and wove into something new, something different. Magickal threads that had stretched one direction turned and shot off in another.

And Cordelia kept speaking.

Angel slashed at the tentacles with the keen edge of his blade. As quickly as he could lop off the end of one, another one would strike at him. They reminded him of cobras he had battled in Asia in the early 1800s, a dozen of them all striking in concert under the direction of a mage with whom there had been a bit of a disagreement. These tentacles, he had found, weren't venomous, but their barbed hooks easily slipped under the skin, and then tearing them free was painful indeed.

He couldn't hope to dodge them all. When one snagged him, he chopped at it. Severed from the god, the suckers didn't hold, and he could yank the hooks out fast, before the next one struck.

All the while, Angel hacked away, weaving a flashing web with the sword. He kept advancing on the god, trying to keep it from extending more of its length out of the pit. It had probably fifteen feet of its body out, and it writhed and wriggled like a giant snake. Now and then it would snap its big teeth at him, or dart out with its tongue, hoping to capture him. But for the most part it seemed to rely on its tentacles, which Angel could see were bunched at a segment break on its trunk, like a shoulder with fifty arms.

The god, he believed, still had more of its length inside the hole than out. Which meant that there could be more shoulders, and more tentacles, to come.

Another good reason not to let it get out. Or fifty good reasons.

He pressed, swinging the sword with abandon. The thing lost tentacle after tentacle, and each time, it unleashed another wail that seemed certain to deafen Angel forever. The stink, too, every time he cut into it, was horrendous. But those were minor nuisances compared to the alternative.

He had been right all along. The real action had been inside the Fletcher house. Everything else had been mere distraction—some magickal, like the vampires who weren't, and some caused by humans foolishly listening to someone who knew just enough to be dangerous. If he let himself think about that too much, he might come to the conclusion that humans were too stupid to bother saving. But then, he knew that only some were so easily manipulated—that others, probably most, were capable of making up their own minds and couldn't be led around by a half-wit with a microphone.

Angel chopped, he slashed, he hacked and hewed. The sword felt like a thousand-pound weight in his hand, the tentacles seemed like flames licking toward him, impossible to defend against. But he tried, and he pushed, and he got close enough to feel the thing's hot, steamy breath flowing through its nostril flaps, close enough to hear the snap of its jaw as it chomped at him. He struck quickly, slicing off half a dozen tentacle ends, and as the god quivered in pain, he lunged and drove the sword into its face, between the nostrils and mouth. The sword sank deep, and pale green fluid that must have been its blood gushed out; Angel withdrew the blade and stepped back.

Angel was in a defensive posture when the tongue came again, and he gripped the sword with both hands and swung down toward it. The blade cut into the top edge of the tongue, and the god screamed, louder than ever, a horrible sound that echoed in the cavernous chamber and that Angel knew would ring in his ears for a week.

As it did, though, its tentacles went momentarily limp, and Angel attacked again. Another stab to the face, another gout of blood. Its tongue came more hesitantly this time, and again Angel caught a piece of it with his blade. He moved forward for another assault and realized that the god was moving—slowly, almost imperceptibly—back toward the pit.

He had done better than stopping its progress, he was actually reversing it.

At the same time, he realized something else. The chasm, the pit from which the god had emerged, was narrowing. Somehow, the hole in the earth was healing itself. The question became, would the god realize it and come out completely before the hole closed—in which case, Angel would surely die trying to fight it? Would it be chopped in half as the hole shut with it half in and half out? Or would Angel be able to drive it completely back inside before it closed altogether?

At the rate it was narrowing, he wouldn't have to wait long to find out.

"Hold it back!" Lorne shouted. He knew the microphone might pick up his voice, but that was a minor consideration. There was almost nothing left of Mac Lindley, just a few shreds of skin that looked like someone had popped a flesh-colored balloon—Caucasian flesh, he mentally added, not the rich, handsome green kind. The goddess's tentacles were wrapping themselves around the microphone cord, trying to pull it back, and Cordy and Wes struggled with everything they had to keep it. Cordy's voice was tight with effort, and Lorne hoped that Wesley's spell didn't actually have to be intelligible to be effective.

They had gone past the holding pattern, beyond just trying to keep the tentacles back long enough for Wes and Cordy to finish. The thing seemed to be almost fully emerged—and the space in the narrow mobile home was much more cramped than it had been, since her bulk was about ten times that of the former radio personality she had used as an unwitting doorway. She was all snapping, gnashing teeth and a darting purple tongue and more tentacles than a herd of octopuses— which he knew was the real plural of octopus, that whole "octopi" thing being a myth—and of course horrific breath that made him wish he was back underneath garbage someplace.

Cordelia was staring intently at Wes as he uttered one of his Etruscan expressions, and Lorne didn't even see the tentacle slithering about her waist until it was too late. When she felt it, she screamed. Connor reacted instantly, darting to her side and severing the tentacle. Goddess blood splashed down Cordy's side, and Connor, a gleam of hatred in his eyes, threw himself right at her.

"Connor, no!" Wesley cried, but it was too late. Connor engaged with her, jabbing again and again at her broad head, at her huge eyes. Tentacles wrapped around him, and her tongue snaked up his back.

"That's it!" Lorne called. "We've got to take her out!"

"But, Lorne," Wes protested, "the spell!"

"If you haven't finished it by now, you never will!" Lorne replied.

"That's just it, Lorne. I have!"

Lorne, Fred, and Connor all stabbed at the goddess, dodging or ignoring the ripping, writhing tentacles. Gradually it sank in to Lorne what Wesley meant: If he had finished the spell, then the portal should be closing—and if it did, they wouldn't want Connor to be attached to the goddess. Poor kid had already spent enough years in an alien dimension for one lifetime. *And I should know,* he thought.

"Cut him free!" he shouted anxiously. He went from stabbing to slashing, trying to cut the tentacles and tongue that the goddess used to hold Connor close to her. Wesley and Cordelia dropped the microphone and joined in the effort.

But the goddess fought back, and she seemed very determined.

Angel thought the tide was turning. He kept advancing on the god, kept slashing at tentacles and taking every opportunity he could to bury his weapon to its hilt in the creature's flesh. The god's wail of agony was interminable, its blood flowed like water from a pump. It even seemed like the strength in its tentacles was lessened—they still hurt when the hooks pierced Angel's skin, but they seemed to move more slowly, and they didn't wrap tightly around his limbs when they caught him.

Inch by inch, foot by foot, he carried on the

struggle. And inch by inch, the god retreated into the pit. Angel pressed on, never giving it a moment's rest, pushing, pushing. For a few minutes he hadn't been sure, had thought maybe the god was just marshaling its strength for another assault, but finally he had become convinced. He was winning. The god was going back down the hole, back into the earth from which it had come.

The god was giving up.

Angel didn't want to become too confident. He didn't want to give the god even a moment's advantage. So he kept up the battle, kept slashing and cutting and stabbing, until the god was completely back in the hole. The god paused for a moment, baring its teeth ferociously but ineffectually, and then lowered itself beneath the rim of the chasm. It was going back down.

Angel had won.

He stood at the rim, watching it sink away. The opening was beginning to narrow even faster, and Angel could see that it would be completely shut in just minutes, if that. The god had to drop fast if it didn't want to be crushed when it closed. Triumphant but exhausted, Angel bent his legs and rested his elbows on his knees as he watched the god's retreat, sword held loosely in both hands.

Watching the god's face, he didn't even notice the tentacle until it twisted around his ankle and tugged.

Angel fell into the pit.

He caught the edge with the fingers of one hand and hung there, suspended inside the pit. The rock walls were coming toward him, as fast as a door shutting. The god's tentacle held him fast, inside the chasm. He still gripped the sword, though. With all the strength he could bring to bear, he lifted his leg, bringing the tentacle to within range of his blade, and chopped at it. The tentacle fell free, just the portion of it stuck into his ankle by the barbs remaining.

Then he hurled the sword down, hoping to score at least one final injury to it, and grabbed the rim with his other hand. He kicked at the wall, but his feet slipped on its smooth surface. The tunnel narrowed rapidly, down to three feet across now, still closing.

Angel pulled up with both arms. His head cleared the rim, then his shoulders. Finally, enough of him was above it that he could swing his legs up and onto solid ground. Just as he did, the earth closed with a boom. When he dared to look at it, nothing was there but smooth, salmon-colored stone, with no indication that there had ever been an opening.

The god was gone. Angel was victorious. For the time being, anyway.

But the god had been banished before, and had returned.

Angel knew that he was going to have to keep tabs on this property. He would have to make sure no one ever tried to build here again.

He didn't want any more innocent deaths on his conscience. He knew he couldn't save them all.

But he could try.

EPILOGUE

The long night was ended, the sun high in the Los Angeles sky by the time everyone got back to the Hyperion. After showers—everyone took showers, so long and hot that Angel worried for the second time in two days about the industrial-strength water heater's capacity—they gathered in the hotel lobby.

"I know I didn't beat it by myself," Angel said. His hair was still wet, and it felt nice and cool after such a long time in the steamy depths of the cavern. He wore a loose, off-white shirt and black pants and loafers. Not monster-fighting clothes, but he didn't intend to fight any more monsters today. "So I was guessing that you guys had somehow managed to close the portal."

"We did," Lorne confirmed. "Well, Mr. Ex-Watcher and Ms. Ex-Higher Being did. The rest of us just kind of hung around."

"As if," Cordelia countered. "If it weren't for them, Wesley and I would have been lunch long before we finished what turned out to be a ridiculously long and tongue-twisting incantation."

"Don't say that word," Connor moaned. He had his back on the floor and his legs up on the banquette next to where Cordy sat.

"Incantation?" she said.

"Tongue."

"She kind of took a liking to Connor," Lorne revealed. "Went at him like a cow with a salt lick."

"Should've figured it'd be English who saved the day," Gunn said. "While I just hung out around town tryin' to keep folks from killin' one another."

"I think the important thing is that it took all of us," Fred pointed out. "Angel might not have beat the god if Cordelia and Wesley hadn't closed the portal. They couldn't have done that if we hadn't been there to keep the goddess off them. And Charles, you were helping keep the peace until we could get things calmed down. None of us were extraneous."

"That's true," Angel agreed. "Plus, we wouldn't have even known what was going on if you hadn't done the legwork, Gunn."

"Yeah, I guess," Gunn admitted.

The conversation trailed off for a moment, and Angel took advantage of the quiet to reflect, now that he'd heard everyone else's stories. What it came down to, he realized, was love. The two gods had loved so deeply, so permanently, that they were drawn together even after the passage of eons. He didn't know if they were really gods, or demons, or what—but they were nonhuman entities that loved just as completely as any humans ever had. The power of love was not limited to any one species, any single life-form. Maybe love didn't conquer all, but if there was a more powerful force in the universe, he didn't want to encounter it.

All they had wanted was to be together.

Angel caught himself staring at Cordelia, and she caught it, too, met his gaze for a moment, smiled, and looked away.

I know how they feel, he thought. *I know just how they feel.*

ABOUT THE AUTHOR

JEFF MARIOTTE is the author of several previous Angel novels, including *Close to the Ground, Hollywood Noir, Haunted,* and *Stranger to the Sun.* With Nancy Holder, he wrote the Buffy-Angel crossover trilogy Unseen and the Angel novel *Endangered Species,* and with Maryelizabeth Hart added to the mix, the nonfiction *Angel: The Casefiles: Volume 1.* He's published many other books, including original teen horror series Witch Season, original novel *The Slab,* and more comic books than he has time to count, some of which have been nominated for Stoker and International Horror Guild Awards. With his wife, the aforementioned Maryelizabeth Hart, and partner Terry Gilman, he co-owns Mysterious Galaxy, a bookstore specializing in science fiction, fantasy, mystery, and horror. He lives in San Diego, California, with his family and pets, in a home filled with books, music, toys, and other examples of American pop culture. More information than you would ever want to know about him is at www.jeffmariotte.com.

As many as 1 in 3 Americans
who have HIV... don't know it.

**TAKE CONTROL.
KNOW YOUR STATUS.
GET TESTED.**

To learn more about HIV testing,
or get a free guide to HIV and
other sexually transmitted diseases:

**www.knowhivaids.org
1-866-344-KNOW**